Hooked on You b)

Hooked on You Copyright © 2015 resides with author Annemarie Brear
First Publication. September 2007 by The Wild Rose Press under the author name Anne Whitfield.
Second Publication: February 2014 by Annemarie Brear at Smashwords.
Cover design by Image: Annemarie Brear

Hooked on You

AnneMarie Brear

AnneMarie Brear

Published novels:

Historical
Kitty McKenzie
Kitty McKenzie's Land
Southern Sons
To Gain What's Lost
Isabelle's Choice
Nicola's Virtue
Aurora's Pride
Grace's Courage
Eden's Conflict
Catrina's Return
Where Rainbow's End
Broken Hero
The Promise of Tomorrow
The Slum Angel
Beneath A Stormy Sky

Marsh Saga Series
Millie
Christmas at the Chateau (novella)
Prue

Contemporary
Long Distance Love
Hooked on You
Where Dragonflies Hover (Dual Timeline)

Short Stories
A New Dawn
Art of Desire
What He Taught Her

Chapter One

London, England 2007.

I had the wild urge to laugh as I stared at my boss, Mr Plunkett, and watched the confused emotions playing across his face. Due to the seriousness of the situation, I bit the inside of my cheek to stop a silly grin from spreading.

Why had I been so nervous about this meeting?

I'd been waiting all morning for him to show up, worrying how he would react, wondering if he'd shout and rage, but he'd done none of that.

His silent shock had been worth a morning of anxious waiting. The incredulous look on his red, perspiring face was priceless, and he was now colour coordinated with his appalling crimson and pink striped tie.

Despite the air-conditioned office, sweat glistened through the few wisps of badly dyed hair left on his balding head. His mouth gaped open and closed like a stranded fish. Oh yes, it was extremely hard to keep a straight face.

'But Miss Edwards, I don't understand…' A look of distaste narrowed his piggy eyes as he glanced at my resignation letter on his desk. 'I...*we*...are a good team!'

Shuddering slightly, I didn't give in to the temptation to say what I really needed to say after months of working closely—too closely—with this horrid, groping, pond-slime worm. He'd taken the meaning of personal assistant to a whole new level. At first, I thought he was just being friendly, fatherly even, but then the light contact with my breast on more than one occasion made me realise there was nothing fatherly about Mr Plunkett.

Shifting in his seat, Plunkett peered at me, steepling his pudgy fingers. 'Miss Edwards, I do believe you must work out a notice of two weeks.' He rocked back in his leather chair with a smug smile.

Prepared for a sneaky tactic, I flourished our contract out from behind my back. 'Not so, Mr Plunkett. The agreement I signed stated that either party could terminate the contract within the first three months without issuing a notice. My three months aren't complete until the end of next week.'

Again, he impersonated a fish, one of those ugly gropers, an apt name considering. It was his turn to wiggle like a worm on a hook, and I was enjoying it. So many times, he'd made me feel uncomfortable. Yesterday's offer of drinks after work, just him and I, had me shaking all the way home. I'd fended off worse in pubs and bars for years. But never to this extent at work.

That was the defining key to this mess. I'd rarely come across an over-attentive boss like Plunkett and I was thrown out of my comfort zone.

Plunkett left his chair and walked around the wide mahogany desk, while I took two steps back. He thought he was something special behind his desk, which he repeatedly told people cost him five thousand pounds. Honestly, who pays that much for a desk? I think it was his way of having a mid-life crisis. Most men went out and bought red Ferraris, Plunkett got himself a smooth mahogany desk with all the trimmings, including a gold-plated nameplate.

'Miss Edwards…' His slick smile didn't hide the lusty look in his eyes. 'I'm devastated. Are you certain you want to leave us? Would you care for some time off? A little holiday, maybe, to help sway your mind? We could go for a weekend away and discuss your needs.' He reached out as though to put his arm around me, and I froze for a second before the trembling began. No job was worth this, especially this shitty job.

'No, thank you. I've cleaned out my desk and all the office paperwork is in order. I wish you and your company continued success.' I didn't actually. The business of debt collecting, was as undesirable as its owner. 'Goodbye, Mr Plunkett.'

I'd made it to the door when he called my name. With some hesitation, I glanced back over my shoulder to look at him one more time. 'Yes?'

Plunkett scratched his flabby jowls. 'I hope we can remain friends? Perhaps we can stay in contact, or come to some kind of arrangement?'

I bet!

'I'm a generous man to those who know me well. You could do very well by me. Would you consider a pay rise?'

I wouldn't.

Opening the door, the tension drained from me as freedom beckoned. 'No amount of money could tempt me to stay. Good day.'

I left his plush office and walked to my small, repulsive and inexpensive plain desk. I hated this desk. There was no logical reason why I should not like a perfectly normal piece of furniture, but I did. Being situated right next to the front door, I couldn't avoid Plunkett every time he came in or out of the office. The other two girls had desks in the far corners of the room. They could hide or read OK magazine behind their computer screen instead of working. I was completely exposed to everyone and at the mercy of the draughts on a chilly day.

None of it mattered now. Halleluiah! I collected my handbag feeling like a prisoner let out of jail.

'We'll miss you, Katie,' Delia, a grandmotherly matron in twin set and pearls, called from across the room. She was an avid listener on Monday mornings to my groggy tales of wild weekends. I don't think she ever had a life.

Turning, I smiled in thanks at Delia and Susan, the only other office staff for Plunkett & Smith, Debt Recruitment. They weren't awful women, but neither had they given me support whenever Plunkett tried on his leaning-over-my-desk-hand-accidentally-brushing-my-breast conversations. Another shudder shook me.

Knowing I was never coming back, some of my sassiness returned and I stepped over to Susan's desk. I had the suspicion she'd been Plunkett's victim before me. 'You know Susan, there are much better jobs out there than this one.'

Her pale face went to ghost white. 'I'm sure there is, Katie,' she whispered, shooting a glance towards

Plunkett's closed door.

'Don't let him bully you. He's a pig.'

All animation and light left her. She seemed to shrivel before my eyes, and I knew I'd been correct in my thinking. Susan looked away, a pink flush creeping up her neck. There was no point in saying anything more, she wouldn't listen. Sadly, she was one of those women who'd never stand up for herself and always accept what was sent her way.

'What do you plan to do now, Katie?' Delia asked, all motherly concern.

'Absolutely nothing for a few days.' I laughed.

'Aren't you worried about finding another job?'

I shrugged, slipping my bag over my shoulder. 'Not really. Something always turns up.'

'You're brave.' Susan sighed, looking like a prisoner on death row.

'Or stupid,' Delia mumbled. 'The young never think of the future.'

I resisted the urge to respond with a sarcastic remark and instead straightened my shoulders and lifted my chin. 'It's been nice working with you both.' I managed another smile at each of them. It hadn't been nice at all. In fact, this had been one of my worst jobs, and I'd had a few. I gave them a final wave, feeling sorry for the poor cows, and almost ran to the front door.

Moments later, seated in my sweltering hot car, I drew a deep breath. Despite the heat of midsummer London, goose bumps broke out over my skin. Now I was free of Plunkett, I finally realised how much his behaviour and my workplace blues had gotten to me.

Bugger that for a joke.

That was the final time I worked for such a bastard. Bosses like him should come with warnings.

After all, it was only fair. We sent out resumes listing all our good points to give potential employers an idea of what to expect, employees should get the same courtesy.

Accept position with care, has tendencies to be a complete bastard.

I laughed. I could always rely on my own strange sense of humour to cheer me up.

God, I was sad.

God, I needed a holiday, and lazy afternoons spent gossiping with girlfriends and forgetting the world at large. Oh, yes!

Excellent idea.

Cocktails.

That would do nicely. Very nicely.

With extreme satisfaction, I carefully reversed my old model Ford out of the car park at the back of the building and headed for Lambeth Road. The only decent thing about the job had been its parking, which saved me from taking the tube.

I hated the tube.

There wasn't anything else in the world I hated more than being in the tube. Travelling underground at speed wasn't human, and after a few hairy experiences with some nutters on an ecstasy high and another occasion when we had a two hour break down, when I thought I'd stop breathing, I promised myself that should I survive that day, I'd never step foot on the tube again, and I hadn't.

Justin Timberlake sang to me from the radio as I drove over Lambeth Bridge. He was the closest I had to a man in my life, which was way too sad to even think about. Where had all the decent men gone? Really? At twenty-eight had I missed the boat? Was there a time frame on finding the best men, say from twenty-two to twenty-six? For the last ten years I'd been partying hard without a thought to my future because I thought it would, eventually, all fall into place.

Did that mean while I was having the odd one night, or the several one weekend, stands and dancing on tables and attending concerts and well, everything else I've been doing, a lot of which I don't completely remember in detail, had I missed the special time frame for women to choose a mate? Had I made the biggest mistake of my life?

I flicked the radio over to another station and George Michael sang to me instead.

Maybe being gay is the way to go.

No, I couldn't abide sharing my bathroom with another woman. I made enough mess for three women as it was, and I liked being the sole person responsible for choosing what chick flick to watch.

Midday traffic slowed my progress but not my sense of relief. I was free of the *Toad*, so things could only get better from now on. The sensible side of me said *you've thrown away a decent job which paid the bills*, but I quickly ignored that side of my brain, which was always so damn boring, and thought instead of the what to do for the rest of the day.

Lunching with friends was out, as they were all at work.

Visiting Mum and Dad and earning a lecture on responsibilities was definitely out.

What did that leave?

Coffee with my crazy sister, if she could spare the time from her hair salon? That didn't appeal to me. Listening to Steph's latest boyfriend gossip grew thin rather quickly when it was always about some loser with a nipple piercing and an aversion to working. No wonder our parents had grey hair and wore worried frowns. Plus, it meant driving to Camden, and as much as I considered myself a nonconformist, most of the people who lingered around Camden freaked me out.

What to do then?

At the traffic lights in Knightsbridge, I fully let down my window, since the car's air conditioning had packed it in months ago. A warm breeze and exhaust fumes hit my face. I watched people eating at a café, whose chairs and tables were placed outside near the road. What possessed people to eat and drink near belching car exhausts? And why were they out in the sun? Did they take pleasure in turning their pale English skin a lovely shade of lobster red?

Still, watching people drink coffee and eat salads made me hungry. I hadn't eaten since breakfast at seven that morning, and it was now nearly one.

On the green light, I drove on towards Kensington's high street past all the shops lining the main street. They seemed to silently beckon. On the left was the dress shop I'd visited last week with Joanna and spent a fortune. Next to that, was a bag shop, and next to that, the cut-price cosmetics store. On the right was my favourite shoe shop. I sighed. *That* was certainly out of the question. Retail therapy would have been just the ticket if I hadn't just thrown in my job. Where the money would come from now, I had no idea. That reminded me I had my credit card bill to pay today.

The large McDonald's golden arches loomed ahead on the right and I smiled. I couldn't really afford new shoes, but six McNuggets and a thick chocolate shake was close enough to a reward. After all, if I didn't get another job soon take-aways would be a thing of the past and I'd be living off baked beans on toast.

The parking gods were smiling on me today as a van pulled out of a space on a side street, and I quickly took his spot. No one ever got parking in Kensington. I locked my car and entered the frantic atmosphere of McDonald's.

While waiting for my order, I considered my options. I had enough savings in the bank for two week's worth of bills, and a fully paid-off credit card. A fortune—no, but it was a safety net. I silently thanked the fates that Christmas was over, and my parents had given their daughters cash as presents. Steph had spent hers within a week on a trip to Amsterdam, but some sixth sense must have known I'd need the money.

I smiled and thanked the spotty teenager who passed me my order. The place was packed, not a spare seat anywhere. It was too hot to walk up to Kensington Gardens and sit in the sun. I decided to go back to my car to enjoy my mini feast in peace and quiet.

My mobile rang as I munched on chicken nuggets. One handed I searched through my bag, which turned into the Tardis from Dr Who the moment I needed something from it.

Just managing to answer the damn phone before it rang off, my voice came out all breathy. 'Hello?'

'Katie, what are you doing?' Joanna quipped. 'You sound as if you've been running, or something just as exhausting. Are you with some fancy guy I don't know about?'

'Huh, I wish.' I swallowed a mouthful of food. 'You know I can never find my bloody phone in this bag.'

'Are you at lunch?'

'No...well, I am eating lunch, but not in my lunch hour, so to speak.'

'You finally walked out of that shitty job, didn't you?' Joanna's voice rose. 'How wonderful. Good for you. He was a dirty old swine.'

'Yes, I know.'

'It's about time you saw sense.'

'Well, it's done now. I don't have to see him again.'

'We must go for drinks tonight. What time?'

'I'm not staying out late. I can't afford it now.'

'A couple of hours won't hurt. We'll go to Tony's bar. There's always guys there who'll buy us drinks.'

I cringed. Tony's Bar was a sleazy pick-up place. It was never my first choice to party. 'No, not Tony's. How about we go to the movies?'

'No, too tame. It's Friday and I've had a horrid week at work. I fancy some fun.'

'And I don't fancy fighting off guys all night. I just escaped one creep.'

'Okay. Leave it with me. I'll ring you later. I've got to go. Miss Stuck-Up-Bitch is bearing down on us. I can hear her heels tapping down the corridor. Kiss. Kiss.' The phone went dead, and I threw it onto the passenger seat.

Poor Joanna. She worked in a job she hated and for a dragon lady boss, who controlled her staff like a sergeant–major. It was only the great wage that kept her there. I was a bit worried about Joanna. Lately she seemed tense and nervy, so unlike her. Despite being beautiful, clever, and sharing a bed with the hunky Lachlan, Joanna wasn't happy. But then, who did I know who was truly happy?

Suddenly the food I ate sat heavy on my stomach.

Life was shit at times.

Here I was, sitting in my wreck of a car on a hot summer's day, eating McDonald's, with no job, no boyfriend and no real future.

What did I have to look forward to? Weeks of applying for boring jobs, interviews, watching my money dwindle, my parents' worried looks, missing out on sales at the shops…

Crap.

Perhaps putting up with Mr Plunkett hadn't been so bad. I mean, I could have done it for a few weeks more until I found another job. Why was I always so impulsive? Why didn't I look for another job first?

Why hadn't I gone to university like my parents wanted and studied for something worthwhile? If I was a lawyer or nurse or something like that, I wouldn't have to put up with dead-end jobs with crap wages.

I really shouldn't start the 'why' argument.

But the truth was I didn't want to be a lawyer or a nurse. I didn't want to do that when I was eighteen and I still didn't want to do it at twenty-eight.

I was feeling sorry for myself.

I gazed around the street. The afternoon was growing warmer. I had hours to fill in until I met up with Joanna. What to do? Go home to my tiny flat and clean the floor or do some laundry? I screwed my face up at the idea.

The phone rang again, the tune of some pop song that I no longer liked. I'd have to change that ring tone. Joanna's name flashed up. I frowned. 'Yes, Joanna? Is something up?'

'Where are you? What are you doing?'

'Eating in my car. Why?'

'Okay, you need to get to Euston Road in an hour.'

'Euston Road in an hour? Are you mad? Why?'

'Gail rang me. You know, my friend from accounts, with the frizzy hair? Anyway, she asked if Lachlan and I wanted to go out for dinner next week and—'

'What's this got to do with me getting to Euston Road?'

'Let me finish, I told her you'd given up your job, and she knows of a P.A. job going at this magazine place. It's through her cousin Jemma, who works there. So, she rang Jemma and Jemma said she'd book you in for an appointment. It's the last interviewing day today. Can you get there for three o'clock?' Joanna finally ran out of air.

'I'm not prepared. I don't have a resume with me, and I'll never get there for three if I go home and get a copy.'

'I'll do one for you and email it over to them. I've got an hour to make you look fantastic on paper.' She laughed.

I laughed, too, and felt blessed to have such a best friend. 'Can you make me fantastic in the flesh too?'

'What are you wearing?'

I looked down at my black skirt and white blouse. Boring office clothes. With Mr Plunkett's wondering hands and eyes, I never glammed up for work. 'I'll put my hair up, and dab on some lippy. I'm decent enough, I guess.'

'Okay, here's the address. Got a pen?'

From my Tardis bag I grabbed a pen and used the back of an envelope to scribble down the address. 'What kind of magazine is it?'

'No idea. But the job isn't working on the mag but being a P.A. to the boss or manager or someone like that apparently.'

'As long as he's not another Plunkett, I don't care.' I smiled.

'Katie, you're going to have to get the tube, you know. You'll not get there in time in the car.'

I swallowed. 'I know, damn it.'

'It'll be worth it if you get the job. Think positive. I'll see you tonight. Good luck.'

After saying goodbye to Joanna, I drove my car down a few side streets and parked it where there was a longer time limit. Taking a deep breath, I started walking towards the nearest tube station.

This job better be mine if I have to suffer a claustrophobic train full of hot, smelly strangers.

Chapter Two

'So? How did it go?' Joanna kissed my cheek and then perched on the bar stool next to me, giving the guy she shoved with her elbow an apologetic smile and a flutter of her lashes.

'It wasn't so bad.' I glanced at her long legs clad in classy black pinstriped slacks. I'd give ten years of my life to be as tall as her. She could have been a model with those legs. Yet, she hated being tall, always complaining men didn't want women they had to look up to. Still, she'd managed to hook the delectable Lachlan, who was as tall as her and genuinely wonderful. Lucky cow.

'And you survived the tube? Amazing.'

'Don't be a funny bitch. Yes, I survived it, though it is still as bad as ever. I had a huge guy next to me and his B.O was revolting. A woman had me cornered with her pram. I could feel my claustrophobia rising.'

'You're so dramatic. It's perfectly safe. People do it all day, every day.'

'And I'm happy for them, but I don't like it.'

'You're such a snob underneath.' She grinned,

took off her suit jacket and laid it over her knees. 'Tell me all about your interview.'

It was six-thirty and the tavern was so crowded people spilled out onto the street. Not that they seemed to mind. Everyone took advantage of the great weather. Friday evening drinks appealed to the masses after a long week at work.

I got the barman's attention and ordered two vodka and oranges before turning back to Joanna. 'There's not much to tell really. Some woman in her fifties interviewed me, can't remember her name, and she said I'd be the personal assistant for the son of the owner, whose name I can't remember.'

'Lord, Katie. You are supposed to at your best in interviews.'

'I was nervous and having a mad dash across the city before it was not the ideal way to prepare.'

'What else?'

'Um, I didn't meet the owner because he was in a meeting. The owner is retiring next year, and the son will take over, along with his brother, or some rubbish like that. Anyway, until then, the job will consist of travelling and obviously pandering to the son's every need, which sounds tedious.'

'That's what personal assistants do, silly.'

'I'm thinking I should apply to work at McDonalds or sell tickets for the London Eye. Something completely different.'

A sarcastic raise of her eyebrow was the only response I got. 'How much travelling would you do on this job?'

I waited for the barman to give us our drinks and then paid for them. 'Don't get excited. It's not Paris or Milan. It's not a fashion mag. The magazine is about *sports* adventure or something like that.' I rolled my eyes. 'I'd likely be travelling to the frigging Amazon to watch my boss canoe down some bloody river while I get eaten alive by mosquitos or leeches or some horrible creature. Or I'll have to trek up the Scottish Highlands in freezing weather and watch him jump off a cliff or shoot a stag.'

Joanna burst out laughing. 'You hate sports.'

'Yes, and I think the woman interviewing me got that impression.'

'What's the bet that your boss would do none of those things, and he gets you to do it while he writes an article about it from the safety of his hotel room?' Joanna gave a wry lift of her eyebrows.

I stared at her, horrified. I hadn't thought of that. 'I'm not jumping off a bloody cliff, that's for sure.'

'Or even worse, you're stuck in a hotel answering phones and collecting his washing, while the boss sends you photos of all the wonderful places he's visiting in the Caribbean or Mediterranean. And I bet he's a thin, little weedy man with an attitude.'

'Shut up.'

'The kind that spits when he talks. You'll have to wear a raincoat!' She doubled up again.

'You are too cruel for words.' I sipped my drink, completely depressed. 'Why couldn't I be a P.A. to a pop star or George Clooney?'

'Because you'd want to do a 'Plunkett' on them.' She grinned. 'You'd be sacked for sexual harassment on the first day.'

'Absolutely. I'd be happy to collect their dry cleaning and send their mothers a birthday card. They could pay me with sexual favours. Imagine being privy to George Clooney's intimate secrets.'

'You're sick, you know that?'

I laughed. 'Oh well, I'll look for other jobs. The

woman said she'd try to ring me by tomorrow afternoon or Monday morning with their answer. I was the last applicant.'

'Did she seem to like you? Asked lots of questions?'

'I don't know if she liked me, to be honest she was so busy the whole time I was there. A dozen people must have knocked on her office door and the phone never stopping ringing. To me, it seemed as though she ran the place single-handedly.' Sighing, I thought of the woman who interviewed me. She'd been so efficient, so *needed*. I felt useless and I left her office with the sense that my life was rather aimless. It was a feeling that had snuck up on me before, but in the past, I always managed to thrust it away. Only this afternoon the feeling stayed with me, disheartening me. 'I don't think I'll get the job, despite your wonderful resume.'

'Well, never mind. You're lucky you inherited your flat and don't have rent to pay.'

'My flat is the size of postage stamp.'

'It's still yours though.' She gave me one of her superior looks. 'You're not paying rent or slaving away to pay off a huge mortgage.'

'Yes, I do, as it's the only luck I've ever had. Apart from that poky flat, I have no assets and no life.'

Joanna's phone rang to the sound of an old Spice Girl's song, and we started to sing to it. I chuckled and sipped my drink. We were such tragics. She quickly turned it off. 'It's only Lachlan.'

'How is Lachlan? He's such a sweetheart.' I indicated to the waiter for another round of drinks. Swallowing the last mouthful of my V & O, I looked at Joanna and sensed her unease. 'What's wrong?'

'He asked me to marry him last night.'

It was my turn to impersonate a fish out of water like Plunkett had done at lunchtime. 'What the hell? He proposed? Why didn't you tell me?'

'I just did.'

'Yes, in a very non-excited way, for God's sake. Why didn't you tell me instantly?'

Sighing, Joanna shrugged, tossed the straw out of her glass, and gulped down her drink. 'I don't want to think about it. I wasn't expecting it. He just did propose last night after we made love.'

'What did you say?' This news was momentous. I couldn't understand her lack of emotion. The hubbub of noise and the crush of people faded from my mind as I watched my best friend pay for another round of drinks.

'I said I'd think about it. I was too shocked to say anything else.' Joanna gave me a weak smile that didn't reach her lovely brown eyes.

Joanna was everything I wasn't. She was tall, dark, and slender, with an angelic face that hid all her thoughts. Me, I was the total opposite and I often wondered why she thought me interesting. I was not very tall, such a bone of contention all my life. I had wavy, strawberry blonde hair, well it was actually dark blonde, but calling it strawberry made me feel better. I refused to call it mousy—I wasn't mousy in any way! I had curves, not always in the right places, or as my father often said, I had good 'childbearing hips,' and I was impatient, impulsive, and a little silly at times. I was forever getting her into situations that should push the boundaries of friendship, but Joanna took it all in her stride. I loved her for it.

'You don't want to marry Lachlan?' Was she mad?

'I don't know. Honestly, I couldn't have been more shocked if he'd said he was suddenly gay or had a sex change or something. We've only been seeing each other for eight months. It's too soon.'

'But he's lovely.' I know if he'd asked me, I'd have said yes in a heartbeat. The sudden thought made me jerk upright. Marriage? I would have said yes to marriage? My God. I wasn't hungering after that, was I?

I always thought marriage was like buying a new computer, we all wanted one, but when you got home the damn thing didn't work as it should. There were hidden codes that no one understood, simple things became huge issues and within two years everyone was looking for a newer model replacement.

Did I still think this was true? I had no idea.

I frowned at my drink, was it a double?

Joanna took a large sip of hers. 'I wanted to ring you but when I looked at the clock it was nearly midnight.'

'It wouldn't have bothered me.' I grasped her hand and squeezed it gently. 'I'm always here for you.'

'I know.' Joanna wiped her face, and her hand shook. 'I can't give him an answer, Katie, and I've hurt him. He expected tears of joy and a resounding yes. All he got was me in shock and a mumbled excuse. I'm such a bitch.'

'You're not a bitch. He's asked a question of you and you're deciding the answer. Marriage is important. You have to be sure. That's all there is to it.'

'It's not how it is meant to be though, is it? Everyone who proposes expects the other partner to say yes and squeal and all that.'

'Not always. Not in real life. We're just used to

seeing it on the telly. You panicked.'

Joanna stared at me, sadness clouding her eyes. 'What would you have said?'

I blinked, thinking of the right words. 'It's not my decision to make.'

'No, come on, be honest. What would you have said if you were me?'

I cringed, knowing I couldn't lie to her. 'Well, you know me, I'm such a soppy bugger, I'd have burst into tears at the idea someone loved me that much.' I grinned. 'You know I'm a sad mare, no one will ever ask me to marry them. I can't even keep a boyfriend for more than a few months before I'm bored.'

'That's because you haven't found the right person. You always go out with boring guys and you lose interest quickly.'

'Maybe.' I shrugged and wished there was more vodka in my drink.

'It's true, and you know it.' Joanna rested her elbow on the bar and put her chin in her hand. 'Do you know how tragic we are? You're searching for Mr Right and can't find him. I have my own Mr Right, one who wants marriage and babies, and I can't decide if I want him.'

'True.'

'I am a selfish fool.' Joanna looked close to tears, which was rare for her.

Marriage and babies.

When did it suddenly get so serious?

When did we suddenly grow up?

Most days I still felt like I was eighteen. How did important adult issues abruptly come into my life?

And why did the news that my best friend could experience all these things first upset me?

'Oh shit! Why did he have to spoil it all?' Joanna

drank the rest of her drink and slammed the glass down. 'We were fine as we were.' She signalled for the waiter. 'Bugger it. Let's get sloshed.'

'We got *sloshed* last weekend.'

Joanna smiled, her eyes taking on the gleam of seriousness that always alarmed me for it usually meant whatever she had planned would happen. 'And we're going to get absolutely rottenly sloshed again this week.'

Chapter Three

The shrill ring of the phone woke me. I opened my eyes to bright sunlight streaming across my bed. Raising my head sent pinpricks of pain darting behind my eyes. I sat up and my stomach rebelled. I stumbled to the bathroom and vomited. The phone kept ringing as I knelt before the toilet bowl and heaved as though it was an Olympic sport.

Finally, the phone shut up and silence descended. My head pounded. No, it didn't pound, it throbbed. My brain was dislodged and banging against my skull looking for a way out. I was dreadfully sick, and it was all Joanna's fault. I was dying because Joanna was scared to get married.

Never will I drink again!

I crawled back to my bed and threw the covers over my head to block out the sunlight. Something caught my eye, and when I looked down, I noticed a purple stain on my white blouse. What the hell? I'd ruined my blouse. A vague memory came through the fog in my brain to remind me of dancing on a street corner and spilling my cocktail. Another image came of me snogging some guy in a wine bar.

Oh, God. I hadn't been that drunk for a while and now I know why. I was a tart when drunk. Too much alcohol made me a tart and made Joanna mouthy and domineering. She picked fights with guys, and I kissed them better. We were lethal.

The phone started ringing again, intent on driving what little sense I had from my head. Groaning, I manage to climb out of bed and make it into the kitchen/sitting room area. Grabbing the phone, I wanted to swear badly to the person on the other end. 'Yes?'

'Hello. Miss Edwards?'

'Yes?' I frowned. I was in pain and my mouth felt like I'd been in a dust storm. If this was one of those marketing callers wanting to sell me a window glazing, I'd scream the ugly swear words even I didn't like!

'This is Karen Leonard calling from ARS Magazine.'

'Oh. Hello...' I sat on the sofa and blinked a few times to focus. The magazine job and the rejection. I didn't care in the slightest. I only wanted my bed and for the world to go away.

'I'm just calling to let you know you've been successful in gaining the position of personal assistant to Mr Kennedy.'

'What? Me? Oh! Really? Are you sure?' For some reason I stood and did my absolute best to act sober, which was silly really because Karen Leonard couldn't see me sitting on the sofa, hung over and dressed in yesterday's clothes. 'Oh, that's great.'

'You're still interested in the job?'

'Er...yes. Yes, very much.' I lied. Right at this moment I couldn't have cared less if I was personal assistant to darling Prince William, or even cute

Harry for that matter.

'Good. Excellent. When can you start?'

'Whenever you need me to.' If she said today, I would simply die.

'Well, Mr. Kennedy is up north on a fishing assignment. Would you be able to travel up there and begin working this week?'

'Um, yes, that should be fine.'

'Excellent. Mr. Kennedy senior would normally want to meet you first and welcome you to the staff properly, but he's travelling to Cornwall this weekend because his mother, who is eighty-five, just had a stroke.'

'Oh, I see.' I didn't actually. In fact, I was very confused. Two Mr Kennedys? Which one was I working for?

'Now, Mr Kennedy, Mr Liam Kennedy, will be your direct boss. It's his affairs you'll be solely responsible for.'

I sat back down and gave up on my act. Rubbing my sore head, I winced as pain throbbed in my temples. 'So, Mr *Liam* Kennedy is my boss and he's up north. Is that right?'

'Yes. He's the driving force behind the magazine, but his last assistant left to have a baby. Do you have an email?'

'I have a laptop, yes. Email.'

'Wonderful. Oh, I see you gave me your email address when you filled out your details yesterday. I'll email your job description and all the personal forms you need to fill in and sign. Can you get them back to me as soon as possible?'

'Today?' I tried to be positive, but the thought of doing paperwork made my head swim and my stomach heave.

'Today would be great. That way I can send it all to Mr Kennedy tonight and he'll know you've been assigned. When can you travel to meet him? All your travel expenses are listed in the documents I'm sending you, and you will be paid fortnightly, but if you need money now to travel north, I can deposit advance travel money in your bank.'

'No, I don't need money advanced.' Was that me who said I don't need money? I was sicker than I thought.

'Good. I'll send all the paperwork right now. If you use your own car, you'll receive a petrol account card, but that'll take a week or two to get to you, or you can use public transport to get up there, and then travel with Mr Kennedy when it suits. Just keep an itemised account of what you spend and all receipts. Mr Kennedy is in Cumbria; the address is in the email.'

I tried to keep up with her, but she was rattling off information faster than a telemarketer. 'Thank you.'

'My number is on the documents, too, and do ring me any time if you need help. I'm Karen, Mr Kennedy senior's personal assistant.'

'Thank you, Karen. I'll travel north tomorrow to meet with Mr Kennedy and begin work.'

'I'll ring Mr Kennedy and let him know to expect you. Congratulations on the position. Mr Kennedy is a lovely man. I'm sure you'll enjoy the job.'

'Thank you. Bye.' I replaced the phone in its holder and sank back against the sofa. God, I hope Mr Kennedy wasn't a groper.

I had a job.

It didn't really sink in. It was all a bit sudden. I'd been looking forward to having a break. Perhaps a small holiday.

Oh, well.

I found my laptop in the bedroom under a pile of clothes, opened it, and connected for my email. While it was doing its business, I laid on the bed and closed my eyes for a moment to ease my brain functions.

When I next woke up the bedroom was full of grey light. Stormy rain clouds covered the sun. My bedside clock showed 5:16pm. I had slept the afternoon away. I hated doing that. I'd never get to sleep tonight now. However, I did feel close to human again, apart from being disgustingly dirty, and I was thoroughly ravenous. Shit. I'd left the laptop on. Through sleep drugged eyes I read some of the documents Karen had emailed, but the effort was really too much.

After some cheese on toast and a cup of tea, I ran a bath and stripped off my dirty clothes. Relaxing in a hot bath in my tiny bathroom in my tiny flat, I grew more enthusiastic about my new job. I was to be a travelling P.A. It sounded a little exciting.

Soaping up my lower legs and wielding a cheap throw-away razor, I made a mental list of destinations I'd been to in the last five years. Each summer Joanna and I, and sometimes a few extra girlfriends, had travelled abroad for two weeks in the sun. Paris, Rome, Majorca, Spain, Portugal and Ibiza...

Last year's holiday blazed into my mind like a branding iron.

Ibiza.

I couldn't help but groan at the thought. Island fun with 'the girls' had nearly killed me. I got revoltingly drunk every night for a week before my body reneged on our party deal and collapsed through sheer exhaustion on the beach in front of our hotel. I woke up three hours later with near second-degree burns. Stupid.

Leaning back in the bath, I watched the floating bubbles. So far, holidays for this summer hadn't been discussed. After Ibiza, anywhere hot with tequilas, sand and sun lotion was out. That left Lapland, Norway, or Russia, and of course staying in Britain. August in either one of those countries would hardly equal exciting or fun. This gave me pause for thought.

A holiday in this country? No. Never. That's what old people did. They went to the seaside for the weekend and declared any place beyond England's shores as alien. Anyway, 'the girls' declared that a holiday wasn't a holiday if their passports weren't stamped. Silly mares. Where's their sense of adventure? The most adventurous they got was going to the Laundromat without make up on.

Suddenly, I was thinking of my childhood holidays. Mum, Dad, me, Steph and our dog Casper went each summer on country holidays. It took mum and dad two days to prepare the caravan, filling it with boxes of cereal and tins of baked beans and powered milk. Then, we'd all watch Dad heave and swear attaching the caravan to our car. We'd drive all day to some remote part of the country and spend a whole week doing absolutely nothing.

How I hated those holidays as a child. Steph and I would fight like cat and dog because we were bored. I'd refuse to use the 'nature' toilet and get clogged up for days. It often rained or we had gale force winds, which rocked the caravan like a cradle. Funny how mum and dad loved every minute of it. Mum would read romance novels on fold out chairs in the sun and Dad would cook sausages and eggs on the little gas stove.

Frowning, I added more hot water to the bath. Actually, those weeks away hadn't been that bad. I mean, everyone did it back then. There were no weeks in Spain and places like that, was there? All my friends went on the exactly same holidays and when school started again, we'd compare to see who had the most tedious time. I guess if I was honest, I could remember some good times, like when Steph and I built a dam across the stream we camped by, and the time Mum made us cook dinner for her and dad. Steph and I did rather well at that. Then there was time dad taught us to fish.

Fish!

I sat up so abruptly at the memory water sloshed over the side if the tub. How could I forget I had done some outdoor sport in my life? That I had once got wet and dirty for the sake of sport made me feel less of a princess and more of a rounded person, who could work for a sports magazine.

Pride swelled in my chest thinking of the holiday when we went fishing. At first, I had felt fishing was only for old men who had nothing else to do and I declined to lower myself to such an undignified pastime. Thirteen-year-olds do not fish. There had to be some written law about it somewhere. Dad and Steph spent hours trying to catch us something big enough to cook; it became an obsession. Each time they came back empty handed I'd sit on my fold out chair with my book and would look superior, thinking that all people who fished were fools. That was until Steph got stung by wasps while using the 'nature' toilet and had to stay in the caravan and be cared for by Mum. Dad had no fishing partner and begged me to help him. Giving in ungracefully, and only after extracting a promise from him that I could read my book, did I agree to accompany him.

I can't honestly say when or why I picked up a

rod, but at one-point Dad asked me to hold his rod while he did something with the hooks and bait. Within minutes of grabbing up the rod the thing began to shake and bend like it was possessed. I screamed, as young girls do, and Dad went ballistic. The whale on the other end of the line dragged me down the bank, through the reeds until I was knee deep in the water with dad yelling for me to reel in. Reel? Huh? After much sign language I grasped the idea and did as he bid. Well, kind of. It was more of me whipping the rod over my head and hoping for the best. To my utter astonishment a fish leapt out of the water and landed flapping at Dad's feet. His grin was the best sight in the world.

Deep in thought, I stepped out of the bath and wrapped a towel around my body.

Fishing.

I was to begin working for a Mr Kennedy, who was currently fishing in Cumbria.

How ironic. Though to be honest I was a tad disappointed Mr Kennedy wasn't fishing in the south of France or sailing somewhere in the Mediterranean. No, it had to be Cumbria, England.

And I was going to be working for a sports magazine.

Who would have thought it? Katie Edwards and sports. Now there was an odd mix if ever there was one.

Adventure Sports Magazine. Was that the name of it? No. ARS. What did it stand for? Karen had mentioned it in the interview. Adventure...no, Adrenaline. I let out a breath, thankful my brain remembered how to work. Adrenaline Rush Sports magazine. That was it.

Nodding to myself, I padded from the bathroom

into the kitchen/sitting room and switched on the kettle for another cup of tea. It was highly unlikely I would get a holiday this year, now I'd started a new job, unless Mr Kennedy took some time off too?

I became inspired. Mr Kennedy sounded like he worked hard for the magazine so he'd surely take a couple off weeks off in August, which meant I could still go on holiday. Maybe.

With this in mind, I rang Joanna, hoping she'd been in as much pain this morning as I had been. It would serve her right for making us drink to forget.

Lachlan answered the phone, and when I inquired about Joanna, he said she was still sleeping off her hangover.

'Can you tell her I got the P.A. job, and I'm leaving in the morning to go up north?'

'Congrats, Katie.'

'Thanks.'

'Will you be gone long?'

I paused, not having really thought about it. 'I'm not sure. I believe my boss travels all over the place.'

'So, you won't be back in London for a while?'

'I'm not sure.' Did I detect a note of hope in his voice? Heat rose in my cheeks. I thought Lachlan liked me.

'Okay, I'll tell Joanna you rang. Catch ya later.' He rang off, and I stared at the beeping phone. Lachlan wanted me out of the way.

Why? We had always got along well in the past. Sadness welled in me. He didn't want me in Joanna's life? Could that be true? It didn't make sense. I'd been Joanna's friend for years before he showed up.

Did he feel threatened by our friendship? Did he blame me for the hangover?

The phone rang and I snatched up the receiver

thinking it was Joanna calling me back, but my mother's voice came on the other end. 'Katie?'

As if it would be anyone else when I lived alone?

'Hi Mum. How are you?' I had the immediate need to splurge out on lots of chocolate.

'I'm good, love. How are you?'

'Fine.' Now wasn't the time to discuss my new employment. I needed chocolate first. Half listening to mum's recount of her day, I opened the fridge. Nothing even close to being chocolate was inside. Instead, I stared at the food I'd bought earlier in the week when I decided to go on a health kick as a result of my new jeans not fitting me. Only, an hour later after buying yoghurts, salads, and fruits, did I realise my period was due. My bloated stomach was responsible for the jean zipper not going up, and not my diet. Although my diet isn't that great most of the time anyway, but I wasn't going to dwell on it now. It seemed such a waste of energy cooking for one person and snacks were so easy to deal with when there were more important things to do—like watching a chick flick or reading the latest edition of OK.

Sighing, I inspected the cupboard contents, which were just as depressing as the fridge's. I craned my neck to see if I'd thrown a packet of chocolate-chip cookies at the back. Nope. All I had was a packet of peanuts, corn flakes, a tin of peaches and noodles. Bugger, bugger!

'Mum?' I broke into her one-sided conversation about Aunt Robyn and her passion for bingo.

'Yes, Kate?'

I winced, knowing I'd been rude, and she was telling me so by calling me Kate and not Katie. 'Sorry to interrupt, Mum, but remember when we went on that fishing holiday years ago?'

'Fishing? Lord, Katie, what are you talking about?'

After some lengthy discussions with Mum, and Dad joining in on the extension, we finally agreed that the fishing holiday was spent in Cumbria, not in Devon, as mum insisted upon.

'Why did you want to know about that holiday, Katie?' Dad asked, his policeman brain never resting.

'I have a new job, Dad. P.A. again. My new boss works for a sports magazine. I have to travel to Cumbria tomorrow.' I sat on the kitchen floor eating low-fat yoghurt butt-naked under a towel.

'Cumbria?' Mum's voice rose several octaves, as though I'd said I was going to Afghanistan to join the Taliban. 'What happened at your old job?' She demanded to know. She could smell a rat at a thousand paces. 'You're never at one place for more than a few months. You must settle down, Katie. Your lifestyle is ridiculous.'

'I'm trying, Mum.'

'You shouldn't have given up on your photography,' Dad butted in. 'You were good at that.'

'Thanks, Dad.' I could rely on Dad to stick up for me. 'Well, I have to go. I've a lot to do before I drive up north and start this new job.'

'Where will you stay?' Mum's tone sharpened.

'In a hotel.'

'Why are driving and not taking the train?' Now Dad's tone held concern. 'I don't like you driving all that way.'

'Taking my car will give me a bit more freedom to come and go.' I didn't tell them that if Mr Kennedy turned out to be another Plunkett then I wanted the car for a quick getaway.

'Can you call in and see us for a quick cup of tea?'

'No, sorry, Mum. Once I get going, I don't want to stop unless I have to.'

'Go carefully on the roads,' Dad said.

'I'm not driving to Germany, Dad. I'm not even leaving England. I'll be fine.'

'Well, rings us when you arrive,' Mum added.

'I will. Love you both.' I hung up and went into the bedroom. I needed to get sorted. As a P.A. I was brilliant at sorting out other people's lives, but when it came to my own I kind of lost interest. The result was chaos.

I tossed the towel in the direction of the bathroom and slipped on my old, cosy, hot-guy-must-never-see pyjamas and got to work on emails. Karen was a marvel of organisation, and I had all the information I needed for my new job at my fingertips. I sent her back the forms she required and then started packing.

I wasn't sure what to take. Would I need a few slinky evening dresses? Or only serviceable, plain office wear? Casual for weekends and smart suits? With a huff, I packed as much as I dared. Since I was driving my car up there and not going by train, I could take extra. On impulse I added my camera. Dad's comment about my photography made me aware I had let a few things slip in my life. Things that had once been important to me. How had my life become such a mishmash of forgotten dreams?

No. I wasn't going to go down that track now.

I didn't want to start examining my life to find all my faults and mistakes. If I wanted to get depressed all I had to do was watch a soppy romantic movie by myself while eating chocolate ice cream covered with M&Ms.

Tomorrow I was driving north to begin a new job.

Surely that was enough to worry about for one evening.

Perhaps this job would be a good one? God knows, I deserved one.

Cumbria. I scratched my head at the thought. How the hell was I going to drive to Cumbria without getting lost?

I let modern technology help.

From my laptop I found The Crown Hotel, Wetheral, which, ironically, is right on the Eden River. The same river I fished with Dad years before. Only then, we weren't in some lovely hotel with hot running water and efficient waiters. We were in a cramped, damp, old caravan, which stank of wet dog.

I printed out a road map and traced the route. Dad would be pleased, as he still thinks I'm sixteen and learning to drive. Is it my fault he couldn't teach me? Is it my fault he nearly had a heart attack when I just happened to have clipped a streetlight? Get over it, I say!

Feeling a sense of accomplishment, I also changed the ring tone on my mobile to the delectable voice of Michael Bublé. Next, I microwaved a frozen dinner and ate it watching the late news. Yes, watching the news was a secret passion of mine, and a secret it would stay upon threat of death.

I don't know why this particular gene was passed on to me, but for some ludicrous reason, I needed to know what was happening in the world so I could grumble about it. Again, this was something about myself that I didn't over analyse in case I scared myself. It just happened to be.

So, apart from my news-watching nerdiness, Lachlan acting weird, and I was likely to get my period in the morning, all was well in my world. I'd left a slime-ball boss, managed to find a new job, and tomorrow I would head to the wilds of England's North West to start my life afresh.

What could possibly go wrong?

* * * *

There is something rather addictive to driving in the country. Who'd have thought it? But obviously it held some pleasure for those tweed and rubber rain boot wearing society who never ventured into the 'big smoke' and now I knew what it was. No traffic lights, pedestrians, road-rage drivers, cyclists, exhaust fumes, road work, or policemen slowed you up in the country. True, there might be the odd tractor crawling down a narrow lane, but the view was so lovely who cared if it took you an hour to drive three miles?

Pulling into The Crown Hotel's car park, I again experienced that self-righteous feeling of achieving something I'd not done before. The drive up country had refreshed me. In fact, I felt it as a new beginning. A fresh start, turning over a new leaf, and all that nonsense.

What a better way to begin a new life than by spend the day driving in the sunshine, windows down, radio on, and singing at the top of my voice, stopping only to buy petrol and an ice cream, and to visit the toilet since my period arrived with vengeance. This last event could easily have turned my mood, but I put a positive spin on it. If I could survive driving all day, begin a new job in unfamiliar territory, and learn to like someone new, all while having a period and not killing anybody, then surely, I could survive most things.

I climbed out of the car, giving it a pat in thanks for not breaking down, stretched my back, and gazed around. Beautiful. A quaint old hotel, lovely gardens, and a car park full of expensive vehicles—clearly the clientele was top drawer.

Leaving my luggage in the car, I went to check in. The young receptionist smiled when I gave her my name. 'Oh yes. We have your room ready.'

'Thank you.' I smiled. Very efficient.

She handed me the swipe key to my room. 'Mr Kennedy left a message for you. He won't be back until about five o'clock, and he asks if you would meet him in the bar about that time, please?'

'Yes. Right. Thank you.' I nodded and looked at my watch. 3:54pm.

It took me a few minutes to retrieve my luggage from the car and take it up to my comfortable room. After a refreshing shower, I rang Mum and assured her I had arrived safely without incident and I listened to her sigh of relief and murmurings that she could now relax with a cup of tea. Anyone would think I'd just crossed the Gobi Desert by camel train. Though truthfully, I was glad it was over, it was rather tiring driving all day when you weren't used to it.

While cleaning my teeth, I wondered what clothes I should change into. I needed to give the right impression from the start. Sophisticated, yet approachable. Only sometimes I managed to look sophisticated yet slutty, which wasn't quite right. I started applying eye makeup and paused with the pencil halfway to my face. I wasn't going on a night out; I was meeting my boss for drinks. The last thing I wanted was another Plunkett situation, so I opted for the toned-down effect—light foundation, mascara and lipstick gloss. I stared at my face in the bathroom mirror complete with a bright light, which made me look fifty-five.

Sod that.

I might not be going on a night out, but I did need some armour. I tidied my eyebrows with tweezers, added eyeliner and then a little colour to my cheeks. With the hair dryer I crunched and fluffed my hair until it fell in waves and I resembled one of those models in shampoo commercials.

I slipped off the dressing gown I was wearing and donned a long flowing black skirt and black high-heeled shoes. I swapped the pink shirt I had selected for a light blue silk blouse and lastly, I added a squirt of perfume. My reflection stared back at me from the mirror. Not bad. I was no Cindy Crawford granted, but I wasn't half bad either.

Taking a deep breath, I straightened my shoulders and lifted my head. This was the first step in a new life. A new boss, new job, new lifestyle. It needed to work this time.

I gathered my bag, left the room and wandered down to the bar. Walton's Bar. Through the windows, the sun cast shadows across the smooth lawns.

Outside, a wedding party were having photos taken. I ordered a light white wine and with that in hand, settled in a large comfy chair overlooking the gardens and willed myself to relax. Mr Kennedy couldn't be worse than Plunkett, surely. If he was, I'd simply climb back into my car and drive home. All I'd have lost was a day's driving. Yet, I silently prayed to some unknown deity that I wouldn't have to go back and face my old life. Not yet anyway…

Laughter floated across the lawns. I suddenly became wistful watching the groom tenderly aid his new bride as they posed for the photographer once more. It looked picture perfect. A white gown, happy people, flutes of champagne, soft music and contented chatter. Weddings were beautiful, full of hope and positive things to come. Tears welled in my eyes. Oh, great. Why now of all times did I have to become soppy and emotional? I must be losing my mind. What with Joanna talking of proposals and now this wedding, my brain was in wedding overdrive.

I took a deep breath and tried to think of something else, but a cheer went up from the bridal party and my throat caught again.

My single status usually never caused me any concern. I'd had relationships in the past, but no man had yet swept me off my feet. I never thought I wanted to be swept away actually. To me, it seemed a little out of control, as though the man had taken not just your heart, but your head as well, and I never wanted a man to rule me.

However, lately, I felt a change in myself and I was losing the battle to fight against it. I tried to imagine what my life would be like with someone in it who loved me and failed dismally. I couldn't visualise the situation because I'd never experienced it. I'd seen happy, committed couples, like my own parents, but so far, the event had eluded me.

Was I really growing up? I'm not sure I was ready to accept the idea yet.

Pausing in taking a sip of my wine, I gazed around the bar. Wedding party guests trickled in, smiling and chatting. One young couple held hands, looking as happy as the bride and groom.

I felt out of place. Alone.

Sighing, I glanced at the time. 4:48pm. I stifled a yawn. I must be more tired than I realised. More guests mingled around the bar, cutting off my view of the doorway. I stood and made my way toward the bar. If I sat on a stool there, Mr Kennedy might find me easier. However, all thoughts of my imminent boss were scattered as I did a double take of the gorgeous demi-god at the far end of the bar.

A guy stood ordering a drink. Not just any guy, but a *man*. He could not be described as anything else. A man who had that 'all together' look. The kind that oozed sex appeal and class. Something, well, actually, there was a *lot* about him gripped me from head to toe. He just looked *good,* from his tailored black trousers to his white shirt and navy tie and the lazy way he hooked his jacket over his shoulder with one finger. It was lethal to my sanity. He resembled Patrick Dempsey, but he was even hotter than him.

This guy wouldn't have been out of place in some swanky Hollywood party, but he looked as if he would be just as happy climbing a mountain. He had the quiet, dignified appearance of those classic movie stars, Cary Grant, Alan Ladd and well...some of those types, whose names escaped me at the minute. He portrayed an old-world charm yet combined it with modern sexiness and suddenly I wanted to be witty and clever and beautiful. Quite simply, I wanted to watch him, absorb his presence, *be* in that presence.

I wanted to be a part of the wedding!

'Excuse me.' A guest smiled up at me, waiting patiently for me to get out of the way of his wheelchair.

'Oh, I am sorry.' Blushing, I shifted aside and then happily resumed staring at the *man*. Nothing on earth could have stopped me—except the man himself. He happened to glance my way as he picked up his bag from the floor. His eyes locked with mine, and I forgot how to breathe. Oh heavens, he was magnificent. Virile, masculine, sex-in-a-suit.

His wry smile melted my bones and quickened my heartbeat.

Like a foolish schoolgirl I turned on my heels and hurried back to my chair in the corner.

Nice one, Kate. Real sophisticated.

'Hello there.'

I looked up. The demi-god was standing beside my chair! Heat flooded into my face.

'Are you Kate Edwards?'

I nodded like a simpleton. He knew my name. 'Katie Edwards, yes.'

'Nice to meet you, Katie. I'm Liam Kennedy.' He stepped forward and held out his hand.

I know if I hadn't been sitting down, I would have fallen. *He was Liam Kennedy!* Every part of my body liquefied as his blue-green eyes crinkled into a skin-tingling smile that was directed at me. ME!

I hesitated to take his hand because that would make him real, solid. Until now, I had thought he was too good to be true really, and just my imagination being silly. When our hands did clasp, I knew the physical contact would shake me, as if I had some second sight or something. His strong hand was warm against mine. Tingles raced up my spine. I concentrated so hard on this touch that I even felt the calluses on his palm.

Liam's eyes locked with mine and I swiftly detected a change in me. I didn't completely understand what was happening, but something had. It was as though it was meant to be, meeting this man, this weekend, at this time in my life.

And, God help me, it scared me to death.

Patrick Dempsey was my new boss.

Chapter Four

I stopped breathing.

My new boss flashed me a brief smile. 'How was your journey up? Did you drive or take the train?'

'I drove the train.' Stupefied, I smiled at his puzzled expression, then like a slap in the face I realised what I had said. 'I mean-I mean I drove my car. Didn't take the train. I drove. My car.'

Oh my God, I was killing him with my intelligence.

Liam glanced at the bar. 'Are you hungry? Shall we go have some dinner? I know it's early, but I've not eaten much today. I've been meeting reps all day.'

I jerked up as though pulled by a cord. 'Yes, lovely. I'm starving too.' A gush of wetness flooded my panties, and I cursed at the savageness of first day period. It seemed the tampon I used hadn't been SUPER enough. Thank god, I wore a slinky panty liner as back up. Still, a trip to the toilet was needed. 'Excuse me, but I need to visit the ladies.' Before he had a chance to reply, I dashed out of the bar like a mad woman, looking for the little sign that would hopefully save my dignity. It would also give me a moment to compose my brain cells, which I seemed to have lost in the seconds it took for Mr Gorgeous to say hello.

Some minutes later I left the toilets, having done what needed to be done. Hesitantly, I headed back to the bar, hoping I'd be calm and sensible when I saw him again.

'Miss Edwards.' Liam stood near the entrance to the restaurant, his smile warm and comforting. 'I've got us a table.'

I smiled, ignoring the way my stomach clenched as he gazed at me, and led the way into the Conservatory Restaurant, a beautiful room, and as its name suggested, it was all windows, which brought the outside into the guests.

A waiter settled us at a table on the right, and Liam asked for a wine list. I glanced out at the pretty gardens and summoned all my courage and wit to get through the next couple of hours.

My hand shook as I fiddled with the place settings, so I tucked them both in my lap and took a calming breath without appearing as though I was taking a calming breath. Nervous? Who me?

'Would you like wine or something else?' Liam asked, scanning the menu.

'Wine would be great, thanks.' In fact, several bottles of wine might help settle me down, but then that could lead to an awkward situation of me wanting to sit on his lap.

I picked up my menu and panicked. I read the words, but they might as well have been in Spanish for all the sense I made of them.

'It looks good. A wide selection.'

'Yes,' I agreed with a quick smile. I was forcing so

many smiles my face ached.

Relax, Katie. He's only a man, just a man like all the others.

But he wasn't. I knew that immediately.

I lifted the menu up to hide my face more. I had never had dinner with a boss before, this was all new territory for me—made worse by my awareness of him in a sexual way. How did one act in these situations?

Be natural.

I tried to think of something to say.

Nothing.

Mind blank, heart racing.

Excellent.

Think, Katie.

The weather? Too dumb.

What then? I couldn't sit here and tell him how my sister was nearly arrested once because she was sitting in her old car outside a bank while it was being robbed and the police thought she was driving the get-away car. I couldn't tell him how I once trod in dog doings and unknowingly trailed it all through my flat until I smelt it, and when I turned around, my carpet was spottier than a Dalmatian. I retched for hours as I scrubbed it clean.

What did one talk about with one's boss? I cleared my throat. 'This is a lovely place.'

Liam glanced around. 'Yes. I like it. I've stayed here before and found it good.'

'I suppose with all the travelling you do all hotels must blend into one another.'

'It can be that way sometimes, yes.' He paused as people passed by our table to sit at the next one. 'I might have the prawns to start with followed by the chicken.' Liam picked up the wine list. 'White wine or are you having steak?'

'The chicken sounds lovely. I'll have the same as you, please.' Lord, didn't I have a brain. Couldn't I think for myself? I dared not meet his eyes and so stared at the menu with the same intensity I gave to a jewellery brochure. What was wrong with me? Anyone would think I'd never been in the presence of a good-looking guy before. I couldn't work it out. I'd even had sex with a few hot guys in my time, so why was I behaving like some silly virginal teenager with a bad crush?

Liam folded his menu closed and placed it beside his cutlery. 'Do you mind if I loosened my tie?'

'No, of course not.'

'Thanks. I hate being trussed up like a butcher's roast.' He grinned, tugging at the knot and then he undid his collar button.

I watched his long, tanned fingers, wishing I could do the job for him. Wishing I could trace a line down his warm flesh. His tanned skin beneath his jaw held the beginnings of a five o'clock shadow. He oozed sex from every pore, and I doubted he even knew it. Heavens, the room was like a furnace, or was it just me?

'I talked to Karen on the phone at lunchtime and she was very happy to give you the job on my behalf.'

I looked into his gorgeous eyes, all thought frozen.

Liam fiddled with his place settings. 'Of course, if you find that working for me isn't suited to you, please don't hesitate to let me know straight away.'

'I-I'm sure it'll be fine.' *Speak, Katie, speak!*

'This job isn't a normal job. Did Karen mention that? I live out of a suitcase, and so will you. Will that be okay?'

'Absolutely.'

'Karen said you were the only one she interviewed who didn't have ties at home. A partner, kids, that sort of thing.' The waiter returned and collected our menus while Liam told him of our choices.

For some reason I felt sad at what he'd said, and kind of a fool. I was the *only* one interviewed who didn't have ties? What did that say about me? I was too damn selfish to let others invade my personal life? Should I, at twenty-eight, have more than what I've got? I had a scary premonition the answer was yes.

Once the waiter departed, Liam smiled at me and then leaned forward over the table, his expression turning serious. 'Your resume was impressive.' I waited for the 'but' to come and it did. 'But this is no office job, not yet anyway. Eventually I'll be tied to the office in London when my father retires next year, but until then, I'll continue to work as I do now, which is travelling for the magazine.'

'Karen explained there was travelling involved.' I wanted to keep listening to him. He not only looked sexy but sounded it, too, his voice deep, rhythmic, and honey smooth. Funny thing was, I couldn't detect an accent, and his dark tan hinted that he wasn't an average Englishman with pale skin. If I didn't know any better, I'd have thought him European. But then, if he spent his life outdoors taking part in sports then he was bound to be tanned. Was he tanned all over? I shivered in the sublime thought that he was.

'The job is travelling. Where I go, you go.'

My fertile imagination gave his innocent words another *dirtier* meaning altogether. Heat rose in my checks. I blinked and focused on what he was saying.

'As I said, I live out of a suitcase. Home is whatever hotel I'm staying at that night. I expect my assistant to be the same.'

48

'I understand.' I nodded eagerly in case he didn't understand that I understood him. Oh God. I was a moron.

'Tomorrow, we'll go through everything more thoroughly. You have brought your laptop?'

'Yes.'

'Good. You'll have my former assistant's PDA too. It has all the phone numbers and contacts you'll need. Since we are mobile from the office, we need to have constant and instant contact with London.'

'Yes.' I cringed. *Come on, Katie, you know how to make conversation.* 'I'm sorry to hear your grandmother is unwell.'

Liam sighed. 'Yes, I hate the thought of her being in any pain. She's an amazing woman. I adore her.'

'Was her stroke very serious?'

'Not as bad as it could have been, thankfully. We have all been spared this time, which is wonderful.'

'Do you see her often?'

'Not as much as I would like. But I make sure I spend every Christmas with the family. We all gather at her house in Cornwall, one of my favourite places in the world.'

'I love Christmas.' Lord, I hope I didn't sound like a little girl. But the fact was, I did love Christmas. I enjoyed the one day a year when you could sit around in your pyjamas until lunchtime, opening presents, eating chocolate, singing carols, then later, having a huge lunch, where you have to undo the top button of your jeans to allow your stomach to expand. And afterwards playing games or watching some emotional Christmas movie.

The waiter returned and poured our wine. I couldn't function. I simply wanted to stare at Liam, and not have to think. Just looking at him was an indulgence, like when you eat ice cream and then lick the bowl. Hmm, licking Liam…I wouldn't go there.

Another waiter arrived with our entrées. Only, I had no appetite. I also got the distinct feeling that Liam was watching and assessing me. Perhaps thinking Karen had made a huge mistake. I'd never had this problem before, this whole tongue-tied syndrome. If Brad Pitt walked through that door right this minute, I couldn't have acted more ridiculous than I am now.

It was so *lame* to be attracted to your boss. Totally not the done thing.

I had the sinking feeling this job wasn't meant for me. I couldn't work for Liam Kennedy feeling like I do. I would embarrass myself before too long. I knew it as sure as I knew my own birth date.

'Have you always done P.A. work?' Liam asked, forking up his food.

'Yes, mostly. I did some odd jobs once I left school. Retail work and stuff like that.' There, I'd done it. I had strung two completely sensible sentences together. How clever was I?

'My last assistant was only part time, as she's married, and her husband didn't like her travelling all the time. It worked for a while, but in the last year my work has tripled as sports have become even more popular for everyone to do. Before, people were satisfied with only watching it on TV, now they want to take part, which is great.'

'Have you always worked for the magazine?' I swallowed my food, not really tasting it. My sole concentration was on Liam. I watched how his mouth and jaw moved as he ate. He looked and smelled as delicious as the food.

'Yes, mostly. My father took over the magazine

when I'd finished school, but he didn't want me to work for him straight away. He encouraged my brother and I to experience new things and work with a variety of people. I worked at some crappy jobs.' He grinned.

'Name one.' I smiled back, sipping my wine, which was light and fruity.

He laughed. 'Let's see… One summer I stayed with my gran down in Cornwall and worked at a local dairy, that wasn't fun. Getting up before the birds and being sprayed with cow dung isn't pleasant.'

I cringed. 'No, I couldn't think of anything worse.'

'The free milk was good though. I lived on the stuff.' He finished his entrée and pushed his plate away a little. 'What was your worst job?'

'Um, a newspaper round when I was eleven.'

'Ah, another early morning job.'

'I didn't mind the early mornings so much; it was the bad weather I hated. Out in all weathers, frost, rain, sleet, and snow. I'd be freezing when I got home and then have to go to school with numb toes.' I shuddered, remembering the cold weather and pitiful amount I earned—money that now seemed close to child labour.

'It's crazy what we do for money when young, isn't it?'

'Yes, very.' I picked at my food, not doing justice to the beautiful meal.

Liam leaned back in his chair, his blue-green eyes watching me intently. 'Later I worked for a newspaper and even did a stint reporting sports for TV. Then I joined the magazine. It was new then, and we all had to work hard to make it well known and get the shops to stock it.'

'So, you must like what you do?'

He grinned and my toes curled at the effect a simple smile had on me. 'Yes, I enjoy it. I'm not saying I want to do it my whole life. In fact, I know I'll not do it forever. After five years of travelling, I'm growing a little tired of it, but it's not going to last forever, and so I want to make the most of it while I can. I won't complain about what I do, as I know most people work tedious or dangerous jobs. I'm grateful for what I do.'

There was no reply to that, or at least my frazzled brain couldn't come up with something. How unfortunate to gain a position such as this, a dream position of travelling, only to find your travelling partner was as sexy as hell and off limits. It was upsetting to find your boss not only strikingly gorgeous, but someone easy to talk to. Did this happen to other people? Was it a coincidence or quite normal? And why did it have to happen to me? Hadn't I had enough employer drama with Plunkett? Didn't I deserve someone dull and kind, maybe incredibly old and grandfatherly?

'You look tired, Katie.'

I jerked up, realising I'd been playing with my food. Liam's tender gaze cut to my heart. Why couldn't he be an unfeeling bastard? That would have made working for someone as handsome as him much easier. Anyway, I thought all attractive men were selfish, thoughtless swines?

Who changed the bloody rules without telling me?

Stupid hormonal tears gathered behind my eyes. 'Yes, I am a bit tired,' I lied. 'I haven't driven all day before. I didn't realise how exhausting it can be.'

'Did you want to go up to your room?' His eyes softened, and he appeared as if he genuinely cared about how I was feeling. 'You can order room service.'

'Actually, I'm not really hungry.'

'Maybe have a lie down?'

'Would you mind?' I desperately need to be away from him to think and breathe.

'Of course not. I shouldn't have bombarded you with dinner and talking the minute you arrived.' That smile of his could win a teeth whitening ad campaign. His parents must have spent a fortune on them when he was a boy. Or was it all that milk he'd drunk at the dairy?

I summoned a brief smile. 'No, it's not your fault, honestly.'

'I just thought it would be nice to get to know each other a little before we started working tomorrow.'

'Thank you. It was kind of you. And I'm sure I'll feel better in the morning.' Yes, when I tell him I wanted to be in his bed not his employ, and therefore, I have to hand in my notice before I even start.

'Good night.' I stood and left the table, throwing an apologetic smile at the waiter who came to gather our dirty plates.

Lord knows what Liam thought of me. Likely, he assumed I was completely odd, and he had every right to be concerned. My behaviour *was* strange, even for me. And, believe me, I'd done some strange things in the past.

Chapter Five

Once in my room I slipped off my shoes and collapsed on the double bed.

Damn.

Bugger.

Crap.

Why did he have to be drop dead gorgeous?

Why did I have to fancy the pants off him?

Why did he have to be my boss?

This was serious. This was terrible!

Sodding hell.

I had the urge to cry and scream. I didn't know if I wanted to be upset or angry, and it was too difficult to be both. Just for once I'd like things to go my way. Was it too hard to ask, for God's sake?

Liam bloody Kennedy was magnificent—kissable, lickable, take-to-bed-for-a-fortnight hot. How on earth would I be able to do my job with such a guy? I drooled like a puppy whenever he was near.

I fell backwards and stared up at the ceiling. Could I be professional and ignore the skin-tingling feelings? Probably not. Tact and diplomacy weren't strong virtues of mine.

Rolling over onto my side I surveyed the room, which was comfortable and decorated nicely in warm hues. It held everything I needed to make my stay enjoyable. Grabbing the remote control, I turned the telly on and searched the channels, anything to take my mind off the current situation. Background noise helped and when I switched to the news, things fell into place. Life went on. Yes, I'd had a surprise, my boss was scrumptious, but it wasn't the end of the world. I could survive it. I'd dealt with a lot worse things.

I slid off the bed and plugged in the kettle. A soothing cup of tea would steady me. An alcoholic drink would have been better, but I'd had enough alcohol poison in my system from Friday, and the last thing I needed now was a liver transplant.

My mobile rang and I snatched it eagerly from my bag, desperately wanting to have contact with home and all things familiar. I was out of my depth here in deepest Cumbria and that was a bizarre sensation for me. I thought I was tough, unbreakable. How little did I know of myself?

It was Joanna and just seeing her name flash on my mobile made ridiculous tears well. Why was I so emotional? 'Joanna!'

'Katie. How's it going?' Her darling voice comforted me. 'You got there safely?'

'Yes. I'm okay.'

'How was the drive?'

'Long.'

'Did you get lost?'

'No.'

'Have you met your boss yet?'

'Yes.'

There was a pause. 'Okay, what's wrong?' The

heightened concern in her tone had me sitting on the bed fighting back the tears. 'Katie? What's happened? I can tell something has.'

'Nothing's happened.'

'Rubbish, it's in your voice. Something has gone wrong, what is it? Do you want me to come up? I can try and find an overnight train or something.'

'No, no, don't be silly.'

'Then speak,' she demanded. 'You're frightening me.'

'I'm sorry. I'm just being silly.' The kettle switched off, but I ignored it.

'About what?'

'My boss.'

'Your boss? What's he done? Has he done something? Jesus, Katie, you do know how to pick them. Has he done a Plunkett?'

'No! No, nothing like that.' *I wish.*

'Okay, you're not making sense and your sending my blood pressure through the roof. Spit it out, I'm not a mind reader.'

'I'm sorry.' I sighed. How could I explain something I didn't understand myself? I took a deep breath. 'He's Patrick Dempsey.'

'What?' Joanna's voice held a suspicious note. She thought I'd lost the plot. Maybe I had.

'He looks like Patrick Dempsey, you know, the actor, only better.'

'Right, so he's good looking. That's a problem because…'

'No, not just good looking. He's, like, the complete package. He's gorgeous, has a body to die for. He's like some freaking movie star or male model. He has beautiful eyes, bedroom eyes.'

'Again, that's a problem because?' Joanna

sounded unconvinced.

'Yes, it's a bloody problem. I can't work for someone like that.'

'Why? Has he been unkind? Arrogant?'

'No, of course not. At least not yet.'

'Well you can't be too careful. Some of those pretty boy types can be such assholes and need to exert power over females to feel like proper men. You know the type. They think themselves above the rest of us poor beggars.'

'Liam's not like that.' I shook my head. Joanna, for all her intellect was sometimes completely thick. 'You need to stop reading those bloody magazine articles that analyse everything.'

'Then explain the issue to me, because I don't understand.'

'I can't work for him because I can't breathe near him. I can't think straight. All I want to do is stare at him.' I groaned pathetically. I sounded like some melodramatic old-time actress.

'So, you've got the hots for your new boss. What of it? You'll get over it the minute he starts shouting that you've stuffed something up. Just ignore it and it'll go away. It happens all the time.'

She made it sound too simple. Me and simple never went together. 'It doesn't happen all the time to me.'

'No, that's true. You usually get the creeps.' She laughed. 'Well, you did want a change this time and you got it.'

'Not like this.' Why wasn't she taking this seriously? This was easy for her, she never had men problems at work. All the males in her office soiled their pants the minute she gave them one of her superior looks. Joanna was never in awe of people, unlike me. She either liked you or ignored you and she made her mind up within nanoseconds of meeting you. I'd seen her in action and was always impressed. True, some people, the ignored ones, called her a bitch or stuck-up cow or ice queen, but those who were her friends were loyal until death.

'Listen, just ignore your feelings. It's just infatuation and do your job. Remember, it could be worse, and he could be another leech.'

'I know, but—'

'There's no buts about it, Katie. Jesus, think about it. You've got a travelling job and your boss is cute. It's every girl's dream. It was also your dream too.'

'It was a crap dream. A naïve dream that I never thought would come true because dreams don't come true, ever.' I felt the panic rise again.

'Calm down. Like I said, just ignore it and you'll be fine.'

'I don't think I can.' I whispered, walking over to the window. 'I just left him at dinner. Just got up and left. I was becoming emotional. I had to get away from him. '

'Oh God, Katie. That was smart. Do try to act the professional, dearest, it does help.'

I drew the curtains closed against the darkening sky. 'I know, I know. He thinks I'm tired from the drive. I feel stupid.' I suddenly had an awful thought. 'You don't think he would have figured it out, would you?'

'That you like him?'

'Yes.'

'I doubt it. Guys can be pretty dumb sometimes. Well, most times.'

'He isn't.' I swallowed back my fear. 'He's not dumb, the opposite in fact. He's been around the

58

world, done everything there is to do. Karen sent me a brief bio about him. He's the kind of person people make movies about. He should have auditioned for the James Bond movies, he'd have got the role instantly.'

'Oh, puleese. Stop exaggerating. Besides, Daniel Craig is unreplaceable.'

'What am I to do?' I whined.

'Stop panicking. Lord, Katie, you're making him out to be superhuman.'

'He is,' I cried. Didn't she understand? Didn't she comprehend the danger I was in? My heart, my whole world had been turned upside down. This wasn't some passing flirtation, I could sense something much deeper than that. I had the hots for my attractive boss. I was swimming in dangerous waters—the whole shark infested, cyclonic waves and Titanic iceberg type of waters.

'Is your period due?' Joanna's snappy attitude didn't help.

'It's here.'

'Then that could explain it.' She sighed heavily, as though dealing with a stubborn five-year-old. I could picture her nodding on the other end of the phone like some wise old witch. 'It's been a roller coaster few days, leaving Plunkett and everything. Why don't you have an early night and see what tomorrow brings.'

'Yes.' I was tired. Behind my eyes ached.

'And buy some vitamins.'

'Okay.'

'And if it doesn't work out then come home. It won't matter.'

'Yes.' I yawned and felt emotionally drained. I went to my luggage and searched for my pyjamas, though on reflection I should have slipped in a flimsy negligee. *Dream on, Katie.*

'What's happening tomorrow?'

'I'm not sure. We'll probably go over paperwork and stuff like that.'

'Real work then.'

'Yes.' What did she mean by that? Sometimes I believed she thought I did nothing but swan around pretending to work. I could be driven and focused when I had the need. Was it my fault that nothing in my life so far had caused me to be as motivated as she was?

'Good. It'll keep you distracted. Go to bed and get some sleep. You'll feel better in the morning.'

'I hope so.'

'Whatever you do, don't panic and don't romanticise everything, you have a habit of doing that.'

'Do I?' I paused in unbuttoning my blouse. Did I? Maybe I'd watched Sleepless in Seattle too many times.

'Yes, you do. You always fall for a guy and make him out to be a shining knight who'll sweep you away to some fabulous life, but in reality, he sells dodgy cars and usually lives with his mum and couldn't commit to a lottery ticket.'

'Wow. That's harsh. Thanks for making me feel better.'

'Sorry, but I'm only showing you that not everything is golden.'

'I think I have worked that out for myself, thanks.'

'Not with fellas, you haven't. You haven't been in a sensible relationship for years, what does that tell you?'

That I'm a lost cause, obviously, and that maybe I should also get a new best friend. Joanna could be too truthful at times. I didn't want her to hold a mirror up to me, but to wallow in pity with me. Isn't that what best friends do? She should be here with ice cream and cake to cheer me up as we spend hours agonising about my situation, she should not be reaffirming my loser qualities.

'I've made you upset, haven't I?' she asked quietly.

'No, I'm fine.' Liar.

'I'm an awful bitch. You should hate me.'

'Don't be dumb.' And I couldn't, no matter what she did or said I always loved her. Yes, she was blunt to the point of bleeding, but she was also my support in true times of need. In many ways we were like olive oil and malt vinegar, and as all good salad dressings are, we bonded well when it mattered.

'I'm sorry, kiddo. You know what I'm like. I think my period is due too.'

That comment right there was a powerful enough reason why I should stay in Cumbria. PMS with Joanna was like stepping into the ring with a heavy weight fighter, who you've just called a wimp. Joanna with PMS was like playing football in a minefield. One minute, for no apparent reason she would blow up and come out fighting. I honestly believed she needed medication, only I never actually say that to her now. I did once and was lucky to survive with my head intact. I soon learnt to shut my mouth.

'I haven't completely pissed you off, have I?'

'No, dearest.' What would I do without her? Life was never dull with Joanna.

'Good. Now have an early night. In the morning you'll be fine. Remember, simply treat him like every other male and you'll be fine. Liam Kennedy is a man, your boss and not the man of your dreams. Keep repeating that to yourself and you'll soon be over this silliness.'

'I hope so. Good night.'

'Night. Ring me if you need me.'

'Thanks, love you.'

'Love you too.' The phone went dead.

I undressed and donned my peach silk pyjamas in slow, laborious movements as though I was ninety years old. And if this weepy unbalanced behaviour was all down to concentrating on the road all day, then I was never driving for more than twenty miles again!

Sleep. Sleep cured everything from hangovers to upset tummies to idiot woman, such as myself, being insanely emotional.

Shit. I forgot to ask Joanna if she'd given Lachlan an answer. See, already the impact of being with Liam was affecting my life. I'd thought only about my reaction to him and not the dilemma facing my best friend. I'll ring her tomorrow.

In the morning I'd be better. I'd be the smart-arse chick everyone knows me to be. Katie Edwards would be back!

Chapter Six

I woke to a grey overcast day, and my first thoughts were of Liam and the evening before. Funnily enough I'd slept rather well. However, after my shower and while I was dressing in black slacks and a grey blouse, the nerves began dancing the Argentine Tango in my empty stomach.

No. Stop this.

I straightened my shoulders and faced myself in the mirror. A clever, smartly dressed woman reflected back at me. I can do this. Just be professional. I dried my hair, cleaned my teeth and applied light make-up.

Grabbing my bag, I slipped everything I needed into it and left the room without pausing to think. Thinking was bad. *Bad.*

Downstairs, I headed for the same restaurant as last night and where breakfast was set up and people where milling. The aroma of fresh coffee perked me up. It was one of my favourite smells. All I needed to do was keep busy and the day would fly by, my first proper working day as Mr Kennedy's assistant.

I was ready.

'Morning, Katie.' Liam sat at a table on the left. A

half-finished breakfast before him. 'Did you sleep all right?' He stood up as I came closer to the table.

What males did this nowadays? I felt a princess.

'Yes, thank you.' My hopes that overnight he'd turned into some ugly Shrek type creature proved fruitless, it seemed. He appeared fresh, smart, his dark hair still damp at the collar from his shower and he looked as sexy as hell. His white shirt, with some company logo on the breast pocket, and denim jeans gave him a casual air. I thought him to be about six-feet tall, but he seemed bigger because of the width of his powerful shoulders and arms. My reaction to him was no less different than yesterday's. Awareness robbed me of speech. Every part of me responded to his nearness. My toes curled, my stomach clenched, my skin prickled, and my heart raced.

Sexual attraction.

Excellent. *Not.*

There was no denying what I felt, but this was subtly different from previous times when a handsome man caught my attention. I frowned, not understanding why. I concentrated on sitting down and looking around at the other guests, anything to not look at Liam.

'What will you have?'

I was hungry, so that was a good sign I was returning to normal. 'Do we have time for me to have a full breakfast?'

'Yes, of course we have time. Our days aren't structured to office times.' His smile was genuine and lovable. Why wasn't this guy married? Perhaps he had someone special? I bet he did. A wife and three kids, and a dog, a big black one he took for walks. Great. I was slobbering after someone already taken.

Stop it, Katie! How could he have a wife and three

kids and a dog when he lived his life travelling?

'I felt terrible last night for boring you when you were so tired from driving. I'm not usually such a thoughtless idiot.'

'No, it wasn't your fault. Please don't worry about it.' I glanced away from his eyes and read the fishing logo on his shirt.

'Well, today we start fresh. Yes?'

'Yes.' I smiled back and my heart banged against my chest. I ignored it. This was work. I was here to *work*. The mantra kept going around in my head. Work. Work. Work.

Liam's phone rang. 'Sorry. I'd better take it. Back in a sec.'

While he was gone, I sorted out my breakfast and dove in. Everything was cooked perfectly, the bacon crisp, the eggs with a soft centre, my coffee hot, and my juice sweet. Without Liam across the table I could relax and enjoy my food as I usually did. I liked food and never understood those who didn't. I only had to smell bacon frying and I was drowning in my own saliva.

It was only after I'd eaten and sat back replete, did I realise Liam had been gone longer than expected. For a while I gazed out the window and finished my coffee, then as the time stretched, I began to wonder if I should go find him. Should I wait or be pro-active and search?

'Sorry.' I swung around as Liam approached. 'That was the office and, as normal, a five-minute call turns into twenty minutes. I got my ear chewed off for not getting my latest article in on time because I rewrote it again and the photos, I wanted weren't available and so on.'

'Oh, not good.'

He sat down. 'No. I have to admit I hate paperwork and technology. That's why I need you. Was everything okay with breakfast?'

'Perfect.' I smiled as widely as I could. He needed me. Cool.

'Good.' From under the table, he brought out a large bag. 'I've brought you the PDA, files, and stuff you'll be needing.'

I took the bag from him and peeked into it.

'Don't worry about it all now, first just get used to the PDA. Karen says she'll leave you alone for a day or two until you've settled in.'

'That's nice of her. I'll need it.'

'In the blue file are all the phone numbers and everything, in case the PDA gets stolen or lost. I've dropped mine into the ocean twice.' He shrugged as though it didn't bother him in the slightest. 'Now that you're here, they'll leave me alone. You'll be harassed by the office all day and not me. They'll want to know what articles I'm doing for which sport and which edition. I must have the articles sent in three months before they appear in the magazine. We have to liaison with the photographers, layout people, editors, and whoever else wants to stick their oar in.'

'Right.'

'You will oversee all sourcing and booking of our travel, accommodation, food, whatever. You'll also be helping me search for new sports, or athletes we can write about. Companies will also talk to me about their brands if I'm in their area, so you'll be contacting them to set up times and photo shoots.' He poured more orange juice into his glass.

'Okay.'

'While I'm interviewing or creating the article, you'll link up with the office for their needs. Most times I'm able to go after what I want, but sometimes the office will do a special feature, say on snowboarding, and then I'll have to focus on that first before doing something I want to do, like scuba diving.'

'So, you freelance the articles?'

'Kind of.' He grinned and drank some of his juice. 'My family owns the magazine, so I have a stake in the profits as well freelancing. There are some magazines in the States that I write for too.'

'I see.' How busy did this man want to be?

'Once the article or interview has been created, you contact the office and then we'll be sent photos to match the theme. Once we've set it out and edited it the best we can, it goes back to London and they do the layout. We proof that as well.'

'Are you the magazine's only journalist?'

'Nope, my brother Gary does it, too, and we have two more freelancers based in America. Gary and I cover Europe and Asia. That's why we're so busy. I need to be writing articles every day, which includes taking part in whatever sport I'm writing about, so the article has some truth about it. I can't do all that and then worry about where I'm sleeping that night.'

In my bed will do nicely, I'm sure.

I froze. Where had that thought come from? I sat straighter and tried to concentrate.

'Bugger this. Let's go and do something.' He stood and smiled down at me. 'I spent all day yesterday talking with local fishermen and visiting tackle shops. Do you fancy doing some fishing?'

'Me? Aren't I supposed to be sorting your paperwork out and things like that?'

He grinned. 'Sod it. We can do more tonight. If you're going to be my P.A., it might be best if you know a bit about the sports I write about.'

'Sure.'

'Have you ever fished before?'

'Once, when I was a girl.'

'Want to try it again?'

'Yes, fine.' Fantastic. It looked like rain and I'd be spending the entire day watching Mr Gorgeous fish and be completely bored stiff.

'Have you brought some casual clothes; stuff that is okay to get a bit dirty?'

'I've jeans.'

'Hiking boots?'

I stared at him. Hiking Boots? Yer, right. I *so* had cause to buy them in Kensington! 'I've got sneakers.' White ones with fancy sky-blue stripes.

'They'll do. We'll get you kitted out later in the week.'

If I lasted that long.

'I'll grab the gear from the back of the car and meet you outside.' Liam walked with me to the stairs and then went outside. I dashed upstairs, went to the toilet and armoured myself against leakage, changed into jeans, grabbed a jumper, and tied my hair up in a ponytail. Catching sight of myself in the mirror, I hesitated. How incredible. First day on the job and I went from looking like a competent office assistant to looking like a farm labourer.

Chapter Seven

I went to meet Liam in the car park and found him rifling through the back of his Land Rover. Within minutes my arms were loaded with the rods and reels, tackle box, boots, wet weather gear, a net, plus a plastic bag filled with stuff that went with all that other stuff, hooks, sinkers, line, a pocketknife and so it went on.

Liam took off his hiking boots and replaced them with rubber rain boots. 'All that stuff in the bag there, I was given yesterday to try out. I met a rep from one of the tackle suppliers.'

I tried to impress him by holding more than I could carry and promptly dropped a rod. It clattered on the ground in a very unhealthy way. 'I'm so sorry.'

He bent down, picked up the rod and inspected it. 'No damage done. Can't be too careful with this brand. I've had them break easily before. Sometimes I think the cheaper brands can do as good a job as the more expensive ones. I've just bought a Diawa Exceler to give it a try.' He laughed. 'As if I need *another* rod. Have you used one of those before?'

'Um...no.' Stunned, I gaped at him, no doubt looking like a rabbit caught in headlights. He obviously thought I understood all this 'sports speak'. He examined the rod and reel again and then glanced at me with a smile while I struggled to look dignified with my unwieldy collection slipping and sliding out of my grasp.

'You going to throw a line in today?' he asked. 'You might as well.'

Blinking, I nodded, hoping to God he meant what I thought he meant.

He looked up at the overcast sky. 'Good day for it. Perfect light.'

Was it? The change in the weather had made me groan on waking this morning. Gone was the sunshine of yesterday. Instead low grey clouds hung just above the rooftops, accompanied by a drop in temperature.

Michael Bublé rang in my bag and I blushed with embarrassment. There was no possible way I could answer my mobile. Apologising profusely, I fumbled with the equipment and in the end placed it all on the ground just as the ringing stopped. Bugger!

Liam picked up his selection of gear. 'It might be better to give all your family and friends your new work number. Save you taking two phones everywhere.'

'Yes, I will. Thanks.'

He looked at me with an expectant smile. 'Ready?'

'As I'll ever be, I guess.'

The walk from the hotel to the river shouldn't have been difficult but with the amount of expensive junk I was lugging I felt like I'd run a marathon. Long grass didn't help and soon I found out how unfit I really was. It might have only been a mile, but my legs were burning, and my lungs were behaving as if I was a packet a day smoker.

Liam walked with the gentle stride of a jaguar, a jacket and backpack thrown over his shoulder with one hand, and easily carrying his rod and a small tackle box in the other hand. I forced my gaze away from his backside and looked out over the river.

Finally, he stopped. 'This is looks good enough.'

Obviously, this part of the riverbank was somehow perfect, whereas the last mile hadn't been, despite it looking the exact same all the way along. Men were stupid.

I dumped the fishing gear onto the grass, not caring how much it cost. A slight misty drizzle enveloped the land. Mist covered the treetops. Typical!

'I'll set the lines up.' Liam at once started fiddling with reels and lines and all the rest of it, while I waited around as useless a chocolate teapot.

Not to be put off and be made to look like a complete city chick, I rescued the rod and reel from under the pile and then searched for the little bag of hooks. Rapidly, it all seemed terribly complicated. My first sense of unease that I couldn't do this started.

I *can* do this! Of course, I can do this. If old men and kids can fish, then I certainly can.

Disgusted at my lack of spirit, and because I was getting damp, I grabbed at the wet weather trousers Liam had given me and jerked them on. They were too long, but after some folding and adjusting I was satisfied. Abruptly I felt the part. Next I pulled on Liam's spare rubber rain boots. I *looked* like an angler! I looked *ridiculous*, but who cares, no one's watching. Except Mr Gorgeous, of course.

'Here,' Liam came to my side and took the rod from me, 'let me help.' His gaze travelled the length of me, and I blushed at his amusing grin. 'Very fetching.'

'Ha-ha.'

With meticulous care I watched and listened as he explained what he was doing, which was threading, tying, and snipping until the 'wobbler' hung nicely. The pretend bait looked a bit silly in my opinion, but who was I to argue with the professional? Besides, if it meant I didn't have to handle something alive and wriggling, I was happy.

'Now, do you want me to show you, or can you remember from before?'

I couldn't remember a thing about how I fished when I was with Dad, but I'd rather die than tell him that. I smothered a groan. God, in no way did I want him standing close, or nearly touching me. Any other time I would have laughed and said 'sure, show me what you've got, big man!' But this guy, *my boss*, with the come-hither eyes and soft smile made me feel achy with want. Not just sexual want, well that too, but personal want. I had to know all about him, but I was *fishing* for God's sake, not at some party wearing a little black number!

Pasting a smile on my face and ignoring my brisk heartbeat, I swept my arm wide. 'Of course, I remember.' Lying idiot that I am, I grinned and waved him away.

With a nod, he settled his equipment down on the bank some metres away. Out of the corner of my eye, I observed him as he readied his line and fiddled in his tackle box. It was then I noticed other logos on his jacket sleeves.

'Do you fish a lot, or do the other sports take

prominence?' If I talked a bit it might take the focus off what I was doing, or not doing in this case. I smiled, feeling shy in his company, which was such a new experience. Me? Shy? Laughable!

'Each sport receives the same space in the magazine. It must be balanced for the readers around the world, but I do have favourites. I hate marathon running but enjoy skiing. Fishing is relaxing, especially if the days before have been hectic. Unless, of course, it's fishing for marlin or other big fish. That's crazy.' He grinned.

The statement sunk in slowly because the effect of his wry grin on me buckled my knees. I wanted to touch him, to have him look at me like that for the rest of my days. Lord, I'm pathetic.

'Is something wrong?'

Blinking, I leant forward in confusion. 'Pardon?'

'I said, is something wrong?' He frowned. 'Can you cast?'

I snapped out of my lust-wallowing trance. 'No, nothing's wrong.' Blushing, I turned away and closed my eyes. Having him so close took away all my intelligence. That wasn't normal. Usually I was the sassy, sharp bird dangling the carrot for some poor, drunken guy at a bar. This was new territory for me, and I didn't like being out of control.

I tested the rod's weight in my hands and plucked up the courage to throw the line out. Standing beside a professional didn't help my confidence at all. I really didn't have a clue what to do. Oh, why did I lie? Stupid.

Swallowing my pride, I glance at him with a half-smile. 'I'm not particularly good at this.'

'At fishing?' Liam kept his head bent, focusing on his line, and I used this time to gather my scattered wits.

Must concentrate on the job at hand—fishing.

I tugged the line, but it was held fast. How did I throw it out, for God's sake?

Liam glanced up. 'Would you like me to help you?'

My heart leapt in my chest. 'I don't want to be a pain. You're here to fish not to be bothered with me. I can go back to the hotel.'

He lent his rod against his tackle box and stepped closer. 'Without even trying?'

'I'm not here to fish. I'm your assistant.'

'True, but it would help me if you got a feel of each sport. It doesn't matter if you're not good at them, but it'll help if you understand the different sports and what I'm talking about. Though sometimes I don't make sense even to myself.' Again, that wry smile of his sent me to heaven.

After he'd inspected and adjusted my line, he handed it back to me.

'Okay, cast.' He paused; his bedroom eyes full of humour. 'You do know how to cast or is that the problem?'

I felt out of breath at his nearness. I couldn't cast. If I was put to torture right at this minute, I'd be lucky to even remember my name. Still, I couldn't let him think I was a total fool. Lifting my chin, I raised the rod.

'Wait!' Liam stepped in and released the catch on the reel. 'Hold the line here. Gently, yes, that's the way.'

Once he'd moved away, I arched my back and flung the rod and line with all my might. I didn't expect to make the perfect cast, but I did expect the line to go out halfway into the river. Instead, the bait plopped uselessly at my feet on the edge of the bank.

In horrified shame, I snatched a look at Liam from under my lashes and saw him fighting back a smile.

He stepped forward once more and took the rod from me. 'Never mind. It's not as easy as it looks.'

Whatever possessed me to think I could fish? 'It's been a long time since I did this.'

'Here, put one hand on the grip, like this.' Liam gave me the rod and as I placed my hand where he indicated, our arms touched. My skin tingled. The scent of his cologne filled my nose and I wanted to snuggle my face against his neck.

He stood behind me, guided my other hand and then showed me how to tilt the rod back. The rod, line, fishing, and the world in general all vanished in a haze of sexual awareness. I felt dwarfed by his size. He spoke softly just behind my ear. I shivered in sensual delight without understanding a word he'd said. My whole body prickled, acutely responsive to his closeness.

'Okay, now cast.'

I did as he asked, but it was a dismal attempt. My intentions weren't focused on fishing.

Liam smiled such an endearing smile I nearly swooned like some Victorian old maid. I seemed removed from my body and definitely from my mind. This craziness wasn't me. I'd always treated men rather coolly in the past, always ready to give them the slip and run the minute they turned boring. However, now, I released that they were just boys, silly boys who helped pass the time. Liam Kennedy was a man—all man—and I wanted him like no other.

He gathered in the line, reset it, and handed it back to me. 'Shall we try again?'

I didn't care what we did as long as he was close.

Nodding, I got into position again and cast. The line went further into the river and Liam told me to let it draw out a bit before securing it. I did this in a state of indifference. Honestly, the Loch Ness monster could have grabbed that bait and I'd have known nothing about it nor cared in the slightest.

My hand limply held the rod as Liam walked away to his kit. I tried desperately to think of something witty and intelligent to say to keep his interest. 'So, what's the biggest fish you've caught?'

I groaned inwardly. How inane. *Wow, Katie, you're on fire today girl!*

Liam did a perfect cast and glanced over at me. 'A Marlin. I was ocean fishing in the Bahamas.'

Naturally, it was in the Bahamas. It couldn't have been anywhere else. What a dream life he led. 'You must have been to some wonderful places.'

'Yes, I'm extremely fortunate. Though my nomadic lifestyle doesn't suit everyone. Sometimes it doesn't suit me. I get a little tired of all the travelling. I must be getting less selfish, or maybe just old.'

I studied him even more intently. Old? Never. He would be one of those rare males that grew old and still looked ten years younger than his real age. To me, he looked between thirty and thirty-five. If he was older than that he was already proving my point. 'So soon all the travelling will end when your father retires?'

'Yes, and I don't know how I'll cope either. Being stuck in an office isn't my idea of having a quality life. But I know it's not for the rest of my life, or even the next five years, and I'm working on a project for the future.'

'You'll not stay at the magazine long term?' The dream job wasn't obviously his dream after all.

'No. I've done nearly six years already, but I promised Dad I'll take over the office for a couple of years until Gary is ready to do his turn.' He did another perfect cast.

The line wiggled a bit in my hand, but I ignored it. 'Will you buy a house in London when the time comes?'

His gaze went to my line in the water before coming back to me. 'No. I'll have to be in the country and commute. The city drives me insane. I have terrible road rage in the city. I can't cope with the idiots on the road and the pedestrians who think they can walk anywhere without looking.'

'It would be hard to give up a life of travelling to live in one place.'

'I think it will be fine. I said the same thing to Dad recently about his life. I mentioned it would be hard for him to give up the magazine, the office in the city, and go down to Cornwall and do nothing.' Liam adjusted his line and then looked back at me. 'He told me he had no intentions of doing nothing, because that would surely kill him. So, he and my mother recently bought a small hotel and restaurant, and they'll run that.'

'How fascinating.' Amazingly, I found that it *was* interesting. He had a quiet unassuming way about him that drew me in. I wanted to sit cross-legged on the grass and just listen to him. The slight drizzle didn't worry me a bit.

Liam smiled. 'Yes, it sounds wonderful. They'll be happy doing that. Mum likes to be as busy as Dad. The hotel is situated with the sea three miles away and a river at their back door. Paradise.' He looked out at where my line bobbed in the water. 'Reel in and check your line. I think your bait will be gone.'

'Oh, really?' I centred on reeling in, and when the hook lay at my feet it was bare. Some fish just got a free plastic meal. 'Yes, it's gone.'

'It happens all the time. Do you want me to bait your hook?'

'No, I'm sure I can do it.' I had to show him I wasn't a complete fool. I fiddled around in the tackle box, searching for the same bait Liam had used before. Several minutes later, I had the bait on the hook and ready to cast. Remembering my previous efforts, I sighed at the thought of making myself look an idiot again. The evil side of me wondered why I even bothered. Being an idiot was something I got top marks for.

'Want any help?' Liam smiled, as if reading my mind. 'I don't expect you to be a professional at everything we do.'

'Good, because you will be sorely disappointed.'

He grinned. 'I'm rather pleased you aren't good; it allows me to look impressive and professional.'

I laughed, liking his sense of humour. 'Was your previous assistant good at sports?'

'Alison? Yes, a born athlete.' He grinned.

Bitch.

'She had a heart of gold, too, and my working life ran smoothly because of her efforts.'

Bitch. Cow.

'You'll do fine though. Don't worry about it too much.' Liam winked.

Great. Rub it in. I've got massive shoes to fill. No pressure there. I summed up a convincing smile. 'Well, I hope I can be just as helpful.'

'I don't doubt it. Alison only worked part time and didn't always travel with me. It'll be good to have someone with me all the time. This job can get lonely sometimes.'

I gazed at the tender look in his eyes and fought the urge to melt into his arms. I would follow him to the wilds of Africa or the frozen Artic if he asked. Alison must have either been on drugs or a secret lesbian not to want to work full time and travel with Liam. Or in love with him.

The thought made my heart thump. What if Alison had the same feelings I did? Is that why she left? Maybe she'd married because she couldn't have Liam. Lord, I could picture myself doing the same thing, settling for someone else, but never quite having the same feelings for the new guy as I did for Liam. How could any man compare to Liam?

Lord, Joanna was right. I was fanciful and I romanticised things. A drama queen complete with diamond tiara. Damn. I was sick. I needed help.

No, I just needed to pull my head in and stop acting like impractical young girl with a schoolyard crush.

That must be the problem.

At school I never fancied any of my male teachers, mainly because they were either old, butt-ugly, sleazy, or plain weird. Now if I'd had a teacher crush at school it would be out of my system, but instead I'm having it now and it's about my boss. It was clear as crystal. The whole man-in-authority infatuation. Therefore, the blame is directly on the department of education—for not hiring decent male teachers for hormonal girls to develop crushes on.

Liam has claimed the honour of being the first man in an authority role in my life, who is genuinely hot. None of my previous boyfriends held enviable positions, or even worked in jobs that I could admire. One guy tinkered with car wrecks, another was a telemarketer for window glazing and one guy thought that if he studied all his life, he'd never have to physically hold down a job.

Liam was a grown up. I never stood a chance. First the first time I was attracted not only physically, but mentally. I was in deep danger.

'Go on. See how you go.'

What? I blinked, my Liam-filled brain not functioning. Oh, he meant for me to cast. For one blessed moment I assumed he wanted me in his arms.

Fantastic. I was not only lusting after my boss, but now I was imagining invisible come-ons from him.

I turned away and concentrated on the rod and line. I had to get a grip on myself. Soon I'd be a jabbering mess.

Depressed at my sad and desperate dreams, I cast the line totally indifferent to how it landed. Thankfully, it went out enough to be a decent attempt. I locked off the reel and glanced up at the grey sky. I really did need a holiday in the sun. Stuff the Ibiza dramas. I needed a week, perhaps two, of walking on white beaches by a shimmering turquoise ocean, with sexy male waiters and…

No, I didn't need a beach holiday. I just needed someone special in my life.

I sneaked a peek at Liam, who was busy recasting. I don't know why meeting this man should suddenly make me think deeply about my life. I always knew one day I'd get married and have kids. But, as the years have gone on, and no man has made a real impact on my heart, I've become blasé about meeting Mr Right. He didn't exist. So, instead I've been enjoying my single status with abandon. There was no harm in that, was there? I mean, women stayed single these days and were incredibly happy. Look at all the career women who didn't get married and have kids until they were in their forties. Maybe that's what fate had install for me?

Twelve years.

Another twelve years of being on my own. That was an ugly prospect. I couldn't stomach all those years of being invited to parties and turning up alone, coming home from work to an empty flat, watching friends get married. How many hen's nights have I been to in the last six years? Eight, nine, ten? I had a feeling Joanna's would be the next one, and then things would change for me. I'd not have Joanna's time as freely as I do now. Instead, I'd have to share her with Lachlan.

Oh, this was hideous.

I glared at the rod in my hand. Is this what fishing does? Gives you hours to contemplate how rotten your life is? Well, if that's the case, you can stuff fishing up the preverbal backside.

'Katie, I think you've got something there.' Liam nodded to my bobbing line, and I quickly re-focused.

The moment I moved; the line jumped as though it wanted to take flight. It was so unexpected I wasn't sure what to do.

'Take up the slack.' Liam set his rod down and joined me. 'Reel in slowly… That's right. Gently. Can you feel the difference?'

With him so close I could feel a lot of things and none of it had anything to do with what was on the end of the line.

The rod bent and jerked and for a moment I concentrated on reeling in. The excitement built. If I caught a fish, that would impress him for sure. Liam helped steady the rod, and I tingled all over at his nearness. Only, as I reeled in, I wondered if what I was feeling was all one sided. He gave me no signals, no hint that he found me attractive, but he was relaxed around me, which was something.

Suddenly a fish jumped clear out of the water, thrashing in an arc before splashing back into the dark water again. I stared in delight as the rod and line behaved like they were possessed. 'Did you see that?' I laughed at Liam.

'It's fighting with you.' He became terribly serious. 'Don't lose it.'

'Oh, I mustn't. I have to show Dad and the girls!' Filled with this promise of taking home a trophy, I reeled it in with all my might.

'Steady. Steady.' Liam's hands enveloped mine as he helped me bring in what I thought to be a splendid-sized fish.

With swift efficiency, he grabbed the end of the line and lifted the fish clear off the water and onto the bank.

'What kind is it?' I bent over closer and gazed in wonder at my gasping, flapping prize. I felt emboldened. A warrior. The successful hunter. Now I knew why men did this. It was harking back to ancient times when the men caught the food for the people's survival.

'A trout.'

'How marvellous. I can't believe I caught a trout.'

Liam nodded with approval. 'Well done.'

My chest swelled with emotion. I wanted to kiss him so badly I thought I would die. 'My dad will be so proud.'

His soft gaze filtered through my euphoria. 'You can't take it.'

Straightening, I frowned. 'Why?'

He bent to pick up the fish and unhooked it. 'It's

not big enough.'

'You're joking?' It looked big enough. Disappointment filled me as I envisaged old men wearing camouflage, hiding in the bushes with binoculars, ready to jump out at us at any minute.

He stood staring at the fish for a moment. 'There are size limits.'

'Limits?'

'Yes. It's illegal to take anything less than twelve inches.'

I jerked. Illegal! God, that's all I needed, to be arrested for illegal fishing.

He must have seen the alarm on my face because he stepped closer and gently touched my arm. 'That's why we release them.' He winked. 'Bend down here and release him.'

I knelt beside Liam at the water's edge and placed both my hands around the fish taking it from him. I lowered the fish into the water gently and let it go. The trout darted away, safe for another day. I would have nothing to show them at home. I'd forgotten to bring my camera.

'Don't worry. You might catch another.'

But I knew I wouldn't. The drizzle had become heavier. I was very wet and cold, my hair plastered to my head. Not a good look.

Liam leaned a little closer, close enough for me to see a spark of devilment in his gorgeous eyes. 'How about we go back to the hotel and have a drink to warm us up?'

In just a few short words sunshine was back into my world.

He was talking to my soul.

A drink with Liam.

What more could a girl ask for? Well, yes, there

was more, but a drink would do just nicely to start with, thank you very much.

We gathered our things, with Liam carrying most of it, and headed back to The Crown.

'I enjoyed today,' Liam said softly with a frown, as though he was surprised at the statement.

'Me too.' Had I? The soul-searching quietness of fishing didn't push my buttons. On one hand I did like being with him, but on the other hand more time in his company only confirmed that I could easily fall in love with this guy.

I slogged on through the long, wet grass feeling miserable. My dream of working for a sexy boss had come true, and it made me think of the old saying, 'be careful what you wish for'.

'One day we'll go fishing and you'll catch something big, I promise. We'll take photos of it to show your dad.'

I nodded but felt terribly sad. He was speaking of the future, when I knew there would be no future for us as a team. I knew deep inside that I had to decline working for Liam before I lost my heart completely.

Chapter Eight

Three mornings later I'm up to my eyeballs in paperwork, emails and phone calls.

After our fishing day on Monday, Liam and I shared a quiet, beautiful dinner where I listened, probably spellbound like a gawky teenager, but we won't go into that, to him telling me about the places he'd been and people he'd met, which were sporting people I had no knowledge off and who could have sat beside me on a bus and I wouldn't have known them as famous. It didn't matter what we talked about really, it was the time spent together that made it special.

Then Tuesday morning arrived and somebody from head office must have put speed in Karen's morning coffee, because for the rest of the day she had me running around in circles until my head throbbed, and this throbbing came without being alcohol induced—a rare thing indeed. The woman was a machine. She sent emails, spreadsheets, contact numbers, and so many other details I knew I'd forget half of what I had to do before lunchtime. While I was chained to the laptop and phone, Liam left to check the local rivers and talk to fisherman and fishing club officials so he could finish his article.

Wednesday followed the same pattern. I abruptly realised that my predecessor had to have been a bloody saint to get all her work done and still have a heart of gold. At the end of an exhausting day I felt ready to murder someone, preferably Karen, but I'd have taken any suitable replacement.

A knock came at the door and I rose from the bed and answered it.

'I hope you like curry?' Liam held up bags of take away.

'Yes, I do, thanks.' I opened the door wider and let him in. 'I'm sorry about the mess.' In dismay I scowled at the paperwork littering the bed, floor, and every other conceivable surface.

'Karen been keeping you busy?' Liam laughed. 'She's very professional.'

'She's a nightmare.' I quickly cleared space off the small table by the window so Liam could put down our meal. 'But she's amazing and knows everything about running a magazine.'

'Yes, a complete powerhouse. Dad would be lost without her; we all would be. I thought you might have had a full day, so take away is easier than dressing for the restaurant. You don't mind, do you?'

'No, not at all. I'm glad you thought of it. I didn't realise the time or how hungry I was until now. I've been creating my own organising system and it's taken the whole afternoon.'

'Well eat up before it's cold. I'm told that this is the best curry in the area. It should be good. I didn't get a Vindaloo, as I didn't know how hot you like your food. So, there's the basic chicken tikka and lamb Rogan Josh, naan bread, poppadums and rice.

Oh, and I got bottled water instead of wine. You don't mind, do you?'

'Heavens, no. I don't drink wine every night at home. I'm happy with a cup of tea after dinner.' Did he think me an alcoholic?

He searched in another bag and brought out two small containers of vanilla ice cream. 'This is dessert, nothing fancy, I'm sorry.' He popped them into the small bar fridge under the TV.

'It's all lovely, thank you.' The spicy aromas filled the room, and my stomach grumbled. I took my food and climbed onto the bed and sat crossed legged to eat it while Liam remained at the table. Funny how comfortable I felt with him after just a few days. 'Did you have a good day?'

'Yes, very productive. I finished the article and edited the interview with the local fishermen. Did the approval come through about the photos I wanted to use?'

'Yes, but they only want two extra ones to go with the main photo. I'll show you…' I got up, but Liam waved at me, swallowing his food.

'No, sit down and eat. It can all wait until later.'

Settling down again, I stabbed at a piece of lamb with my fork, then switched on the telly to catch the news. As we ate, we discussed various news items as they appeared. We both agreed the legal system needed an overhaul, as did immigration and education. Between us, we managed to put the world to rights within the time it took to share a curry and ice cream, and, with a laugh, we realised we were missing our vocations as politicians.

I couldn't describe my delight at being able to share my 'news passion' with another. Every other man I dated couldn't have been less interested in world events if they'd tried. Some goons I'd gone out with seemed to have only recently evolved from caveman status and didn't care what China was doing or why we should care about buying home grown food to support our industries.

Anyway, those other guys were dweebs compared to Liam and not worth another consideration.

This was our fourth night together, and we were so relaxed with each other that neither of us had to stand on ceremony. We'd eaten together, worked together, and over the last few days formed a good partnership. I was surprised by how quickly we'd gelled. We were becoming friends as well as work colleagues. My heart swelled at the thought. Yes, on my part there was also the undercurrent of sexual attraction, which I fought continually, but sometimes I had the feeling it wasn't *so* one-sided as I first thought. This confused me to no end.

I still had intentions of leaving this job, but the time frame to do it grew hazy. I thought to see how the first week went, but that might not be wise, for Liam was sneaking into my world increasingly with each hour that passed. I woke up each morning with the firm resolution to go home that day, but then meeting Liam at breakfast, with his welcoming smile, undid my good intentions every time. I simply couldn't utter the words that would take me away from him.

I was damned if I stayed and damned if I left. I now just had to work out which action would hurt less, and while I was working that out it was nice to be in his company. 'What are the plans once we leave Cumbria?'

He tore off a piece of naan bread. 'We head to Scotland at the weekend or probably Monday. Can you book us into somewhere in Perth?'

'Of course. What is the sport?'

'Curling.' He grinned.

'Curling… As in that broom sweeping game on ice?' I chuckled. 'I saw it on TV once, and it looked strange.'

'It's a sport in the Winter Olympics and Perth is famous for it. So, we're going to go curling.' He smiled, humour dancing in his eyes.

'Have you done it before?'

'Nope and I'm guessing you haven't either. So, we can laugh at each other.'

'We'll both be trying it?'

'Absolutely. I told you, it helps if you try the sports too.'

My eyes widened. How wonderful. We'd be learning something new together. I felt as excited as a child at a circus. 'Then I'd best study up on it.' I glanced at my laptop and silently thanked the people who invented the Internet.

'After Perth, I think we'll be off to the south of France and white-water rafting. I have to check with the head office first though, because white water rafting has been featured before, and we need to make sure enough time has lapsed between editions before we can feature it again.'

'White water rafting looks like fun.'

'It is.' Liam stretched his arms behind his head and then rubbed his eyes. 'Then we have canoeing in north Wales. I try to do all the water sports in summer.'

'Makes sense.'

'Since we've got the fishing article done, I thought we'd move on to something else tomorrow.'

'Oh?'

'Yes, perhaps we could go hiking.'

I nearly choked on my mouthful of water.

'Hiking.' I forced a smile. 'Great.'

* * * *

I woke up the next morning and lingered in bed making myself believe that today would be a good day, though it was hard to be positive. Liam's ridiculous suggestion that we go hiking in the mountains of the Lake District swamped all my natural happiness.

Hiking.

Yes, bloody hiking. Who thinks up these sports? Even the word 'hike' sounds gruelling. What kind of person wakes up one morning, sees a mountain and says, 'I'm going to walk up that today.' They needed to get a life obviously or their head examined. I have the same kind of tolerance for marathon runners. Those people were insane, truly. What would possess someone to run for miles for no apparent reason?

I remember watching on TV once, a marathon woman runner who had become so exhausted she lost the coordination of her legs. I felt ill witnessing her collapse and then her crawling over the finish line. Honestly, someone needs to tell her she could get the same mindless feeling having a good night out, and you didn't have to train for months before hand.

Sighing, I pushed the covers back and climbed out of bed. I'd been happy to stay at the hotel, but Liam insisted I do the hike. And I did promise to try each sport as he wished me to. I shouldn't have agreed. I wasn't staying in this job, so why do something as stupid as a hike up a bloody mountain? I've got nothing to prove to anyone.

A knock came at the door. Breakfast. Today I'd planned to have breakfast in my room and dive straight into work. Liam had shot that plan to pieces. Opening the door, I bent and retrieved my tray from the floor in the hallway and set it down on the small table. My nose wrinkled at the smell of old curry containers, which filled the rubbish bin. The poor housemaids would have a grumble about that. The room was like a bomb had hit it. Why hadn't I noticed it last night? I blushed with embarrassment. Liam had eaten his curry surrounded by my mess. It wasn't only paperwork, but my suitcase was open, disgorging clothes over the floor, shoes, bags, and make up seemed to have multiplied on arrival and taken over the room. What must he think?

After quickly finishing my breakfast, I swept around the room tidying up faster than Mary Poppins. This morning Liam was having the Land Rover serviced at a local dealership, an appointment I made on Tuesday, so I had time to myself before our great adventure.

Once showered, I changed into jeans and a pink long-sleeved shirt and placed a thick cardigan near my bag. You could never tell what the weather might do up north. The sun shone outside, but it was surprising how quickly cloud could come over. Knowing my luck, we'd get halfway up the mountain and the heavens would open and I'd look like a drowned rat. Not the image I wanted to present to Liam.

The mayhem and novelty of the last few days had prevented me from thinking about home, of missing my old life. Yet, strangely, I didn't miss London. I realised I'd thrived on the fast pace of the last two days. This job was nothing like working for Plunkett. Liam was the total opposite to Plunkett too, which wasn't a good thing for my sanity. After our fishing expedition, Liam had left me alone during the day, most of the time, while he wrote in his room, or he went on drives around the countryside. We'd meet up for dinner in the evening, like last night, and spent the time discussing work before retiring to our rooms.

I don't know what it was about being in the country, but I was tired by nine o'clock and wanting to curl up in bed. It must be the fresh air, lack of exhaust fumes or something, because normally at home, I'd be up watching the late news.

A tap on the door broke into my thoughts. I opened the door and smiled at Liam. 'Good morning.'

'Morning.' His wry smile sent tingles across my skin. There must be a law somewhere that states good-looking men can't have lovely personalities too. As a complete package it's too hard for the female heart to deal with. I keep waiting for Liam to be an asshole, but it hadn't happened yet, damn it. So far, he's been the perfect boss, the perfect gentleman and, for frig's sake, it just isn't natural. With him being Mr Perfect I found it harder to look for reasons to give him as to why I must leave.

Why can't he make it easier on me and be a normal guy and do something to piss me off?

'Is the Land Rover fixed?' I wanted to kiss him so badly I had to grip my hands behind my back before they reached out to him.

'All done. Are you ready?'

I stared. 'Ready?'

'To go to the Lake District and hiking, like we arranged.'

'Oh, yes, yes of course. Give me a minute.' I spun back into the room. He had to think of me as a space cadet sometimes. Honestly, my attention span lately has been zero and went into minus when he was in the same room.

'I bought you these.' From a bag he brought out a large shoebox and placed it on the bed.

I frowned. 'What is it?'

'Well, I might be a bit simple, but shoeboxes usually hold some kind of footwear.'

'Ha-ha.' I gave him a sarcastic smile and opened the box. Hiking boots. Bugger. There was no going back.

'Now you'll look the part.' He grinned with a smug schoolboy expression.

'You didn't have to do that.' He so didn't. The thought of hiking up mountains made me breathless, and we hadn't even left the hotel.

'I guessed your size, but if they don't fit, we can take them back to the shop on the way.' He watched me sit on the bed and put on the boots, which did fit, but felt funny to me. I'd not worn these types of boots before. My feet seemed heavy and unwieldy.

'They fit fine. Thanks.'

He grimaced. 'I shouldn't have bought them, should I?'

Seeing his expression of doubt made me want to hug him in reassurance. It touched me that he'd go out of his way to help me fit in with his work. 'Don't be silly, it was thoughtful of you.'

'I wanted you to feel the part, and joggers don't give the correct support. You could twist an ankle. But I should realise not everyone has the same enthusiasm as me when it comes to some sports.'

'You're very kind. Thank you.' Face heating with embarrassment, I went over to the little table and collected my bag, cardigan and camera. When I went to collect the files, Liam stopped me.

'No, don't take all that. We won't need it. This is a

pleasure trip as well as research.' He took the camera from me. 'Are you good at photography?'

'Not bad. I studied it at collage. I used to enjoy doing it a lot, but for some reason I stopped.'

'I might get you to take some photos for the magazine. You'll get paid and the acknowledgment for them if used.'

'That'll please my dad. He says I should never have given it up.'

'Maybe you shouldn't.' He gave me a direct look, and I wasn't sure what to make of it. In fact, last night at dinner I caught him more than once looking at me oddly, his expression questioning, before returning to his normal self. Was he having second thoughts about hiring me?

Lord, was I crap at this job?

Perhaps being a P.A. wasn't in me? Perhaps I needed to change my career choices and stop applying for the same type of job?

'Shall we go?' Liam opened the door.

I followed him out and down to the Land Rover in the car park.

As we left Wetheral and headed south, Liam switched on the radio and relaxed into his seat. 'Have you been to the Lake District before?'

'Once as a child. I don't remember much of it and I'm not sure where exactly we went.' I stared out the window at the passing countryside. I liked what I saw. I'd had the same feeling when driving up from London. The area deserved its praise.

A shiver went down my spine as in the distance the mountains rose majestically skywards. From here, they seemed to be blue and purple. Breath taking.

Liam stared ahead. 'This district is my favourite part of England. Actually, it's my favourite part of the world. I was thinking last night I'd like to buy a house here, but I'm not sure my future plans allow for it. Though it'd be great to spend the summers in this area.'

'Like Beatrix Potter.'

Liam laughed. 'Well, I can't draw to save my life.'

'Miss Potter is one of my favourite movies.'

'I've not seen it.'

'Why? Because it's a chick's flick?'

'No. Mainly because I never get the chance to watch movies…' Then he fought to suppress a mischievous grin. 'Well, yes, because it's a chic flick.'

'You should broaden your mind, Mr Kennedy. It's a beautiful movie about Beatrix Potter and how, after the man she loves dies, she moves up to this area. Her family had a summerhouse here. She buys up old farmland to save it from the developers.'

'I'll have to watch it.'

'Which part are we going to?'

'I thought we'd go to Keswick and do a short hike of about six miles. What do you think?'

'Sounds good.' I dare not look at him in case he saw the horror on my face. Six miles. He wanted me to walk six long miles.

Walk.

Six miles.

Why? Honestly, who would think walking six miles would be fun?

'If you enjoy it, we can do another longer one tomorrow.'

'Great.' I plastered a smile on my face and kept staring out the window. He was testing me, that was it. Did he expect me to hike two days straight? I'd be lucky to survive this day, never mind do a longer hike tomorrow. Was the man mad?

'You don't have to, of course. You might hate it.'

'I'm sure I'm up to it.' I know I'll hate it. For a start, these boots felt like they were made of concrete. I'd never warn anything so heavy.

'Hiking is a fantastic way to exercise.'

'I can imagine.'

'And six miles is nothing.'

'It's not a walk in the park either.'

'You'd walk more than that around London when the sales are on, wouldn't you?'

I twisted so fast in my seat; the seatbelt jerked to hold me still. 'What is that supposed to mean?'

'Nothing. A joke.' He grinned and shrugged one shoulder, watching the road.

'Are you saying I'm unfit?'

'No.'

'Then what?' Did he think me fat? I know I wasn't as slim as I was last year. For some reason I'd slipped from a size ten to a twelve overnight, and if I was honest, fourteen was on the horizon. Did women get fatter the closer they got to thirty? Was it some kind of hormone imbalance?

'Nothing. Forget it. My humour obviously doesn't work on you.'

'Humour? More like a cheap shot.'

'Okay, then tell me, what do you do for exercise?'

I groaned silently. I hated questions like that. So, I wasn't a health nut, did that make me a bad person?

'Do you exercise at all?' Liam persisted, a cheeky smile playing around his kissable lips.

'Er, yes…'

'What do you do? Or am I being rude to ask?'

'I…um…I walk.' Thank God for that. I thought for a moment I wouldn't be able to think up a suitable reply. 'Yes. Yes, I walk.'

'How much? How far do you walk?'

I could feel my cheeks burning and I stared out the windscreen. Lying wasn't something I did well. Steph had that particular gene. She had a degree in lying and what's more, people believed her lies. She'd got us both out of many scrapes in our childhood by her ability to lie with an angelic expression on her face. 'It depends. Oh, and I run sometimes.'

'Run?'

'Yes, I often have to run for the bus.' I detested running and nothing got me more fuming than a bus pulling away when I was only metres from jumping on.

'Oh, Katie.' He burst out laughing, which annoyed me as I was being serious.

I spared him a lofty glance. 'You find that funny?' I could see him fighting not to laugh anymore. 'It might be wise for you not to ask a girl what exercise she does. It's not very gentlemanly.'

'You're right. It's not my business what you do.' He chuckled some more. 'I'm sorry. I'll keep my mouth shut from now on.'

Damn right. I should have said I had wild sex, as everyone knows that burns calories. *That* would have swiped the grin off him.

He gave me a heart-rending smile, and all mock hostility left me. What I wouldn't do for just one kiss from him. Why was it that when a man apologised, we had the urge to kiss them better, to make them feel less guilty? I never understood that.

We'd been driving for a while, the silence stretching between us, though it wasn't an uncomfortable silence. 'How long will it take to get there?'

'Not long, about another twenty minutes or so and we'll be in Keswick.' Liam searched through console and pulled out a stack of CDs. 'Put on one of these if you want.'

I flipped through the small collection. Queen. AC/DC. Fleetwood Mac. Robbie Williams. I decided on Queen and placed it in the CD player. 'You have similar taste to me.'

'Really?'

'I have these same artists in my collection. You're just missing Coldplay. Oh, and ABBA.'

'ABBA?'

I pretended to be surprised. 'Not an ABBA fan? I feel sorry for you.'

'I'll try and rectify my inabilities in music taste.'

'One night I'll take you to a Karaoke bar, and we'll sing an ABBA song. You'll be hooked for life, I promise you.'

'That sounds rather tempting,' he said.

Tempting? *He* was tempting. This—being so close to him—was tempting. the spark in his eyes made me all tingly with want.

What had possessed me to say such stuff? Did I have no common sense? I needed to leave his job because of my growing attraction, yet here I am suggesting we go out one night and have some fun. I was cruel to my heart, teasing it. They'd be no Karaoke bar, no fun. Liam was my boss, not my boyfriend. It was ridiculous of me to think any different.

Liam shifted in his seat, and I hoped I hadn't embarrassed him. He cleared his throat. 'I'm having to start my collection all over again, as this car was broken into in Glasgow last year, and they stole what CDs I had plus some equipment.'

'That's terrible.' Good, let's get back to mundane subjects that had nothing to do with lust.

'The police think it was kids, because they didn't want the car.'

'My sister had her car stolen, she never got it back. I'm not actually sure why the thieves took it, the damn thing didn't always go. Steph was relieved it went, I think, it saved her from worrying about it.' She enjoyed being able to chat with him. Few men had made her want to talk and share.

'My first car was an old Morris Minor. I loved that car.'

'Did it have the timber trim?'

Liam shook his head in amusement. 'No. It was plain green. A horrible colour green actually, but it worked well.'

'I've only ever had the one car—the one I have now. When I first got my licence, I drove Mum's car. Then after my sister and I moved into the city, I didn't bother buying one. Then two summers ago, I fancied a little car to give me some freedom to travel to my parent's home and things like that.'

'Freedom is a precious thing. How do people survive relying only on public transport?'

'I don't know, but they do, especially in the cities.'

Liam slowed and turned right. 'Do you read books?'

'Not as much as I should, I guess. In the summer I like to read outside under a tree. My parents' back garden is right on the Thames River. Do you read?'

'A little. Sometimes the weather can be rotten, so I'm holed up in a hotel room with nothing to do.'

From now on you can call me to help pass the time. I hurriedly pushed that thought away and searched for something intelligent to say. 'I have enjoyed a few books in the last couple of years; actually, I read a lot more when I was younger. Now I don't always have the time. My mum gives me books, the ones she's liked, and I'll read those.'

'Do you like movies?'

'God yes, I live for the cinema and usually go once a week with my friend Joanna.'

'Once a week?' A shocked expression crossed his face.

I gave him a look full of attitude. 'Yes, I know I have a problem. I'm an addict and I should get help for it.'

'You are funny.'

'Thank you.'

'So, what's your perfect day? Going to the movies?'

I thought for a moment. My perfect day. What did make an ideal day for me? 'Once, this was years ago, a group of girlfriends and I packed up a picnic and drove out into the country. We had a fantastic time. The weather was perfect, the food yummy, and on the way home we stopped at this really old pub in some tiny village and had a few drinks. I remember we seemed to laugh all day. That was a good day.'

'It sounds it.'

'What's your perfect day?'

'Believe it or not, something similar to yours, only I'd like to do it on a canal boat.'

'Oh, I'd love to holiday on one of those.'

'You've never been on a canal boat?'

'Never, but I always wanted to. I like the idea of just cruising along, stopping when you wanted to. On TV they look to be idyllic and romantic.'

'I went on one in France. It was great fun. I spent two weeks cruising canals with some friends, but I'd like to do it again without my drunken mates spewing over the side. That kind of ruins the relaxing surrounds.'

I laughed.

Liam gave me a friendly wink, and I sighed happily. He was good to be with, funny and charming and intelligent. He ticked so many boxes on my Mr Right list it was scary. Each day I was getting to know him better, and I loved it, but where would it all end? He was my boss. How could he ever be more than that?

As we started to wind up through the mountains, we sang 'Another One Bites the Dust'. It surprised me that Liam sang. I'd never known a guy to sing in the car before. It should have been geeky, but me, being lust ridden, found it extremely sexy. He didn't have a good voice, which made me adore him all the more and when he grinned at me, I thought I would self-combust. It'd been a long time since I wanted a man as badly as I wanted Liam, and even longer time since I fancied a man I couldn't have.

I concentrated on singing with Freddie Mercury and absorbing the beautiful countryside as we passed. This seemed like a day out, not an employer/employee exercise. Funnily enough, I was more content at the moment than I'd been in a long time.

Chapter Nine

There comes a time in everyone's life when they are faced with something that will push them past their limits of endurance.

Mine was this bloody hike.

Liam had said the climb had a slow, but steady rise. If that was so, then why did my lungs burn as though I was breathing fire? We had two vastly different ideas about what a 'steady rise' actually is. Every muscle I had ached. In fact, some muscles ached in parts of my body that shouldn't have, and it alarmed me as to why that area should be affected. I understand sore leg muscles, even the odd stitch, but I hurt. Everywhere. My arms ached, my chest ached, my neck and back. I was sure I needed hospitalisation and an oxygen tank on wheels beside me. For certain, if I was a smoker, I'd be dead.

But like the trooper I was, or being forced to be by my own vanity, I struggled on behind Liam. The only pleasant aspect about this whole effing hike was the view right in front of me — Liam's backside. He had a good body, there was no argument about that, but his bum, clad in old, comfortable jeans, hit the jackpot for me. I focused on his bum to stop thinking about the pain racking my body and my laboured breathing.

Liam, being a fit healthy guy, was naturally finding this easy. He was even *talking* as we hiked up the frigging mountain! He was loving this, pointing out places of interest and different things. I couldn't give a toss. I just placed one foot in front of another and silently apologised to my heart and lungs for making them work so hard. Why did people do this to themselves? It wasn't natural and certainly not healthy. This sport was a heart attack waiting to happen. If people wanted to see the top of a mountain, then the sensible thing to do was hire a helicopter. Problem solved.

'We're nearly there.'

If I had breath, I would have cheered.

We walked, or more accurately I stumbled, for another few minutes and then Liam stopped and placed his small backpack on the ground.

'What do you think?' he asked. 'Worth it, isn't it?'

I straightened from my wheezing, hunch-backed position and gazed around, and, despite my agony, I quite simply fell in love with what I saw.

My heart seemed suspended between beats, either that or I was having a heart attack. Whichever. I didn't care. Without a doubt, the scenery before me was spectacular. Beautiful mountains cradled the Derwent Water below. Sunshine bathed the area, highlighting the colours and shimmering on the water like a thousand crystals.

'Want a drink?'

A drink? I needed a bloody swimming pool. But I smiled and pretended to be fit and having a ball. 'Yes, thanks.'

Liam gave me one of the water bottles he carried, and I drank greedily.

He removed his sunglasses and ran his hand through his hair. 'It's good to see the sun out. You'll be able to take some good photos.'

The clear air filled my lungs and made everything pristine. Now that I had my breath back, I could give attention to the beauty around me. I did want to take photos, lots of them, to capture not only the scenery, but this perfect day, and my first hike. For the first time since meeting Liam, something had managed to take my mind off him. Well, sort of.

Liam took my camera from the backpack and handed it to me with a wry smile, as though he understood my thoughts.

I nodded, not wanting to talk, just to absorb the feeling I had. Moving away, I pushed my sunglasses onto the top of my head, made the camera ready, and then indulged in the long-forgotten passion of taking photos. My breathing became regular as I took shots from different angles. I walked around, letting my instinct come into play for which angles to take. I listened to the silence, felt the soft breeze on my face, and wanted to cry from the experience. I couldn't explain my emotions. Never had I been so touched by the wonder and gentle beauty of a place. She'd always be thankful to Liam for showing her this amazing place.

'Katie.'

I turned, dazed, and smiled at Liam. 'Thank you for bringing me here.'

He took a step closer, his gaze roaming my face. 'I'm glad you like it.'

I stared at his lips, silently begging him to kiss me.

I so wanted to be held and loved, especially here.

Liam touched my arm, and instinctively I leaned towards him. Our bodies were so close, I could feel the warmth of his breath on my skin. Was he feeling the same sensations as me? Did he want to touch me, to feel my lips on his, my hands slipping up to thread through his hair?

I sucked in a breath. Desire throbbed inside me. I wanted nothing more at this moment than to be in his arms. Liam's gaze lingered on my lips, and he took a step closer. My stomach clenched in anticipation. For one wondrous moment I thought he was going to kiss me, but abruptly he stepped back a pace and looked away, slipping on his sunglasses again.

'If you've taken enough photos, we'd best keep going,' he said.

He'd seen the passion in my eyes.

He'd known I wanted him to kiss me.

And he'd rejected me.

The cool brush off scenario. No problem. I can handle rejection. I'm an adult. All I had to do was pretend it didn't hurt. Easy.

He collected the backpack and began to make the descent. 'It's downhill now, much easier going for you.'

Thank heavens for small mercies.

'I thought we could grab some lunch in Keswick before heading back.' He didn't wait for me, and I sighed. I had ruined everything.

Those ridiculous emotional tears filled my eyes again, and I blinked hard before covering them with my sunglasses. Damn. Shit. Bugger. How stupid of me to let my guard down.

I slipped the camera cord over my head and started after Liam, who was putting a good distance between us. He had to be embarrassed. Who could blame him?

I replayed the moment again in my mind. Had there been any hint or spark from him? Surely there must have been. Or did I only hope there was? I couldn't remember. I'd been too intent on his lips, and on my own needs and desires.

At the bottom of Walla Crag, Liam waited for me to catch up. 'Okay?'

'Yes, of course.'

'Good.' He walked on. 'We'll be able to get something to eat in Keswick. I fancy some fish and chips. We could eat them by the lake if you want.'

I glanced at him in surprise. He ate fish and chips? He wasn't a complete saint or a health freak after all. 'I'm hungry as a horse,' I said.

Not a very ladylike statement but the truth, nevertheless. All this exercise and fresh air was making my stomach think my throat was cut. 'I can take some more photos too.'

At the edge of the village, Liam suddenly stopped and turned to me.

I stared with my heart in my mouth. I watched the emotions play on his handsome face. What had I done? I'd made him uneasy in my presence and that gave me a pain in my chest.

'I was thinking that you might want this weekend off to go home and sort out things, see family, that kind of thing before we head off to Scotland.'

Ouch. Brush off number two. It was as clear as if he'd hired a plane to write it in the sky above. He wanted me gone.

'But I thought we were heading to Perth straight away?'

'I can go on ahead. You can meet me later. I'm betting you didn't pack enough stuff for constantly being on the road, so this will give you a chance to organise a few things.'

I managed a small smile and nodded. 'Sure. Thanks.'

Well done, Katie. This time you've made the boss want to get rid of you instead of sleep with you.

Why couldn't I get it right for once?

We found a fish and chip shop, ordered, and then took our food down to the lake's edge. The scenery was just as beautiful down here as in the mountains above, only not as quiet. Liam and I ate and spoke a little, mainly about the town and what we saw around us. The atmosphere was tense between us and I hated it. It upset me more to know I was the cause. I didn't need to go home for any reason, and he must have known that, but I could hardly have refused. He clearly wanted some space.

I'd never fancied a guy before and been refused. That's not to say I think of myself as some hot temptress or anything, far from it. I'd fancied plenty of blokes before and never got with them, usually because they simply had no interest in me, were married, or they didn't know I fancied them, which is how I wanted it to be with Liam.

Only, now it was too late. He had a clear idea of my feelings.

Although I'd been hungry before, the tension robbed me of my appetite. My fish and chips went largely untouched, and I threw them in the bin. My desire for food this week had been close to non-existent. Looking on the bright side, this state of affairs would hopefully help me shed a few pounds.

I left Liam sitting on the park bench, eating, and went to the water's edge to take photos. I took my time, not wanting to go back to the awkwardness between us, but neither did I want the day to end because once we returned to the hotel, I would be packing.

It was stupid of me to have stayed so long. I should have left Sunday night when just seeing Liam for the first time knocked me for six. How did I think I would cope working for a man who only had to smile in my direction, and I became a quivering bag of yearning?

Perhaps it was only pent up sexual frustration?

It had been a while since I'd had sex. I paused and lowered my camera. When was the last time I had sex? For a second I couldn't honestly remember, but then it came to me. Last summer, I slept with a guy Joanna introduced to me. We got terribly drunk, and he stayed behind at my flat when Joanna and Lachlan left. One thing led to another and we ended up in bed. The next morning, I felt ill at the thought of what I'd done, not that he wasn't nice, he was, but once was enough. I was glad when he left without staying for breakfast.

Last summer. A whole year. Well, that could explain it.

'Ready to go, Katie?'

I turned and nodded.

In the car, Liam turned the radio on, and we drove back to Wetheral without speaking. I felt uneasy and very conscious of him sitting beside me. From the corner of my eye I noticed the way his hands moved on the steering wheel, how his legs moved changing gears. On the outside he appeared calm, but I sensed his mind was whirling as much as mine. I had embarrassed him. Humiliation cursed through me like a wildfire. I stared out the wind, my cheeks flaming.

It was nearly five o'clock when we arrived back at

the hotel. In the foyer, Liam hesitated by the stairs. 'I'm going to do some fishing this evening. So, don't wait dinner for me; you eat when you want.'

'Okay. I am pretty tired. I might order room service. Happy fishing.'

Happy fishing? What kind of thing was that to say? I was losing brain cells by the day. Liam was definitely giving out signals now. He'd rather go fishing than have dinner with me. Boy, that sucked.

I headed up the stairs, wincing as my muscles ached at more activity.

'Katie?'

I stopped halfway up, and I glanced down over my shoulder at him. 'Yes?'

'Do you fancy going horse riding tomorrow?'

'Horse riding?' What the hell?

'Yes. Would you like to?'

'Sure.' I'd ride a bucking bull if it made the awkwardness leave us.

'Good, I'll make the arrangements. See you in the morning.' He gave me a long look and then walked back outside.

I went to my room in a complete state of confusion. Didn't he, only an hour ago, mention me going home? Now he wanted us to go horse riding? Which one of us was mad? Probably me.

Once in my room I ran the bath, intending to soak away the soreness from my poor legs. Sitting on the side of the bath, watching the water, I pondered again on the day's events. Liam had been cool towards me since we left the top of the crag. I hadn't imagined that. So, why now the invitation to do another sport with him? And why such a physical activity? Did he enjoy seeing me suffer?

I couldn't figure it out. One minute he was cool

and distant, the next warm and friendly handing out invitations to spend more time together. Did he want me to go or stay?

What did I want to do?

There wasn't any clear answer.

Unless he was trying to push past the embarrassment, ignore my signals and simply smooth over the awkwardness so we could continue working together.

Yes, that had to be it.

I was good at my job. We got on well, when I wasn't being lust-struck.

Pretend what happened today didn't happen. Well, if he could do it so could I. From now on I'll treat him like a stranger, or a distant relative at best. I'll think of him as nothing more than a boss. I'll ignore his gorgeous looks, his charming personality, and his intelligent conversation.

I'll be polite and do my job. I can do that.

Easy.

Chapter Ten

Flossie's large brown eyes stared at me in quiet harmony. I stroked her soft nose and chuckled as she nudged me for a treat.

'I don't have anything, beautiful,' I crooned to the animal. 'I'd have brought something if I'd been thinking.' I loved the smell of leather, true it was usually new leather boots, a slinky leather belt, or a classy bag, but the smell of saddles and harnesses was also nice. I liked listening to the sound of hoof beats and the jingle of the bridles.

Exhilaration built in me at riding a horse, and Flossie's gentleness made it more enjoyable. I stroked her neck in long, slow movements. I'd liked to have brushed her. I couldn't understand why I wasn't nervous. Perhaps what mum said last night on the phone had meaning?

Last night, as I soaked my poor body for an hour in the bath, Mum had rung, and I mentioned the horse riding. She told me I'd ridden a pony when I was a child while on holiday in Yorkshire. I'd been five at the time and both mum and dad said I took to it better than Steph. Dad had gone as far to say I was a natural in the saddle. He'd also reminded me that up until the age of thirteen I had ridden the donkeys at the seaside every year. Couldn't get enough of them. His words brought back happy memories. Unfortunately though, after gaining the all-important status of a teenager, I became aware that riding donkeys was not cool and had to be placed in the same category as wearing your slippers outside, riding a purple bicycle with streamers on the handle bars, and kissing your parents goodbye in front of friends.

'Are you ready to mount?' A kind woman came to my side and checked the stirrup strap. She looked to be in her early thirties and had a warm smile. She was dressed in pale jodhpurs and a thick green vest, despite the weather being fine and warm. I quite liked the look of jodhpurs and wouldn't mind a pair myself.

'Yes, I'm ready.'

'Flossie's a good girl, nice and quiet. She'll give you no trouble so keep the reins slack and you'll be fine.'

'Thank you.' I sucked in a deep breath. Here goes nothing. I lifted my booted foot and placed it in the stirrup. My leg muscles hurt in protest after yesterday's hike. If nothing else after this week, I'd have lost some weight. All this exercise and no large appetite would do wonders for my waistline. I'd easily go from a size twelve to a ten, especially if Liam stopped bringing ice cream to me room at night. Nah, what the hell, I'd rather have Liam and ice cream than fit into size-ten jeans.

I heaved myself up and, apart from a whish of her tail, Flossie didn't move. 'Good girl,' I whispered to Flossie and myself. Falling off wasn't on the agenda today. Making an ass out of myself was out of the question.

The stable owner patted the horse's neck before moving away. 'When you're ready, guide her over to the gate with everyone else. She knows the routine and will follow the others. Enjoy your ride.'

'Thank you.' Once settled in the saddle, I gathered the reins in like a professional and turned Flossie's head to the left. As smooth as silk she walked over to the others waiting to go through the gate. Oh, this was good.

'You okay?' Liam came up beside us, mounted on a large brown horse.

'Yes.' I automatically straightened my back and shoulders, my mum's words as I was growing up came back to haunt me, *posture, Katie, posture.* I hoped I looked the part, because I certainly felt it. I flashed him a cheeky smile. 'I spoke to my parents on the phone last night and Dad says I was a natural at this as a child. I rode donkeys at the seaside like I was born on the back of one.'

He laughed. 'Donkeys, hey?'

I ignored the jibe and lifted my chin to give him one of those superior looks Joanna had perfected. 'You look like you've done this before too.'

'Once or twice.' He grinned that playboy grin, which sent my heart into palpitations.

Once or twice my backside. He sat the horse like a young John Wayne. I bet he was a bloody show jumper, or something just as impressive. It seemed this man had no end of talents — a complete athlete in every way. Bastard.

Somewhere in his God-given brilliance he must have a flaw, some tiny detail that made him human. I just had to find it, then he'd be off that bloody pedestal so damn quick he wouldn't know what hit him. Until then, I'd cope with putting up with him and his outstanding ability to be great at everything.

Today he wore black jeans, a blue t-shirt, and a cowboy hat, and to complete the picture he'd not shaven this morning and had stubble. I hoped to God I wasn't drooling because he looked like some sexy cowboy stud straight out of a rodeo advertisement. I wanted to pull him off that horse and have sex with him on the dirt.

This wasn't good. The promise I'd made to myself to think of him as a stranger wasn't working. When he talked to me or even glanced my way I wanted to smile. He made me feel wonderful and keeping emotionally distant was frigging hard. No woman could resist Liam Kennedy. And if she said she could, she lied. It was like saying George Clooney didn't have sex appeal, or Tom Jones wasn't Welsh, or David Beckham couldn't kick a ball.

The general movement of horses indicated we were about to start. As Flossie stepped forward, I glanced at Liam. He smiled back encouragingly, and feeling ten-foot-tall, I relaxed into the saddle to enjoy the morning.

For a while, the small group of us rode together across the fields. Liam rode beside me but talked to a woman rider on his other side. Funny how secure I felt with him staying close. I was surprised I didn't always need his attention and that just having him nearby settled me.

In the car this morning we'd talked of business. He mentioned the plans he was making for future articles, the places he thought needed to be visited, the sports to focus on. I'd listened and took notes, making comments where necessary. It'd all been professional, but it was also extremely comfortable too. The tension between us from yesterday was forgotten, at least by Liam, and I was doing my best to not think of it either. I liked listening to him, learning about him. However, it was becoming harder to not reach out and touch him.

We started to climb across the fells and the beautiful scenery opened out before us. I couldn't believe the beauty of the area. After yesterday's hike near Keswick and now today, I was thoroughly awed by the splendour in this part of England. In fact, I was ashamed that I had given my own country such little interest when picking holiday destinations. The magnificence of the Lake District stirred something within me. I wish I had realised it before. It would be easy to live up here, surrounded by all this beauty and serenity.

I frowned, realising that I didn't miss London. This upset me.

Why didn't I miss London and the life I had there? That *is* my life.

Joanna, I missed, my own personal things in my flat, I missed, but there was no deep longing to return to the city. To say I was shocked by this new awareness was an understatement. I thought the city was my life. I was a true city chick, wasn't I?

How did a person go from being a city dweller to a country bumpkin in the space of one week? Maybe the countryside casts spells on the uninitiated? All the clean air, the peaceful tranquillity of open spaces and slow pace of life is like a detox when you're used to exhaust fumes, rushing around, crowds and slaving your life to a clock.

'How are you doing?' Liam asked, bringing me back to the present.

'Loving it.' And I was. I found that horse riding suited me. Who'd have thought it? Me on a horse being perfectly calm and serene. The girls would be hysterical at the sight. In another life I think I owned a horse; how else can I explain the thrill and ease of this ride? The gentle rocking of the horse's step soothed me. It's too gushy to say it feels like 'I've come home,' yet I can't describe it any other way.

Our guide, the husband to the woman who helped me mount turned in his saddle and pointed. 'That huge mountain is Skiddaw.'

I breathed in deeply, wallowing in the splendour. What a magnificent place to live. The sun warmed my back and if I was any more relaxed, I'd be asleep.

'Were you like most girls and wanted a pony when you were little?' Liam adjusted the reins in his hand and scratched the horse's mane.

'Yes, desperately. My mum tells me I asked for a pony every Christmas from the age of five until I was ten.'

'I can see you as a girl, with pigtails and freckles?'

'Sadly, that's true too.'

'Braces?'

'No, not braces, thankfully.'

'Are you going to try and trot?' Liam grew serious. 'You should, at least try it once.'

'Yes, I think I will.' I felt adventurous. The reality was likely I'd fall and break my silly neck, but nothing gained and all that...

'I thought you might.' He gave me a steady stare. 'Nothing much scares you, does it?'

I shrugged, not wanting to read too much into his admiring look. 'I'm not fond of spiders, but I'll give most things a go. Though I will never bungee jump.'

'It's fun actually, when you've done it once then the next time is easier, and you can enjoy the freefall better.'

I screwed up my face, not believing him for a minute. 'I'll take your word for it.'

'Not going to try it?'

'Never.' I cringed at the thought. 'I'd rather charm a snake than jump off a bridge with only a bit of elastic around my ankles.'

Grinning, he leaned out of his saddle closer to me. 'You should never say never, Katie.'

Somehow, I managed not to reach out and kiss him. Oh God. I was never going to survive this man. Taking a deep breath, I forced myself to be calm. 'I'll stick to horse riding, a lot safer. So, how do I trot? Is it hard?'

'No,' he said with a laugh. 'Lift your bum up on every other stride. Watch the horse's right front leg. When she lifts it up, you go up and come down on the next. It's a controlled lift. Understand?'

'I think so.' I looked over at the guide who again swivelled in the saddle.

'We'll go along Overwater,' the guide pointed to the left, 'and those who want to trot, or canter can do so along the flat.'

Nervous, I gripped the reins. 'I might fall off.'

'I doubt it.' Liam's confidence in me was comforting. 'You look comfortable. You have to use your leg muscles when riding, you can't just sit there.'

'So, it's not as easy as it appears like in the movies?' I joked.

'No. You'll be fine. It's all about rhythm.'

The horses seemed to sense there was a change in pace once we were along the water's edge. Flossie's ears twitched and some of the riders broke into a trot and passed us.

Liam's horse also broke into a trot and Flossie

decided she would too without giving me warning.
'You okay?'

I bounced on the saddle in a most painful way. I
looked nothing like the others, more like one of those
dogs with the bobbing heads people put on the back
shelf of their cars.

Liam, ahead of me, turned around and came back.
'No, Katie, go up and down. Lift your bum off the
saddle as her right leg lifts off the ground. Grip with
your thighs. Count. One, two. One, two. That's it.'

The only thing I wanted to grip with my thighs
was his waist, but I did what he instructed. The jolting
became smoother until I was rising and lowering in
time with Flossie's gait. One. Two. One. Two.

'See, I knew you could do it. I think your dad's
right, you are a natural.'

'Thanks.' I couldn't stop grinning. I'd done it. I
was trotting. A well of emotion and happiness
bubbled up inside me. I felt invincible and very, very
clever.

We trotted along the water steadily as some of the
others cantered away. They looked good and I longed
to join them, but I settled for trotting on this first
outing. I had in mind the idea to take lessons, because
without a doubt this wouldn't be my last horse ride. I
was converted.

Horse riding was my new addiction! Well, next to
my new boss, of course.

I slowed Flossie to a walk as we all turned for the
stables. I didn't want the ride to end and could have
gone on for hours, though I imagined my backside
wouldn't thank me if we did. I knew come morning
I'd be stiff, in pain, unable to walk properly, and
cursing Liam Kennedy in R-rated language.

However, I smiled at Liam as he came alongside

me once more, my heart swelling at his admiring expression. 'I've had a wonderful time. Thank you for suggesting it.'

'Good. I'm glad.' He played with his horse's mane for a moment and then looked at me again. 'So, we can strike this off the list of things achieved? First hiking and now horse riding.'

'Yes.' I chuckled, feeling blissfully relaxed. 'Though I prefer horse riding over hiking.'

Liam gave me one of his sardonic looks. 'I promise the next time we hike it won't be up a mountain, okay?'

'All right then.' There would be a next time. His confirmation of us working together and lasting more than this week gave me warm tingles. He wanted me to continue as his P.A. Did I still have to leave this weekend and go home? I wanted to ask but chickened out.

'I think I'm going to have fun teaching you other sports. I think you can be converted into a sports nut.'

'You think so, eh?' I laughed, loving the friendship, which had developed between us. 'What happens if I become better at some sports than you?'

He shook his head, amusement in his eyes. 'That'll never happen.'

Such a typical male answer. 'I wouldn't be too sure about that. And remember, never say never. I might be a female, but I'm not completely useless. I could become incredibly good at some things.'

His eyes darkened. 'I'm sure you could.'

Was there double meaning in his words, or just my imagination and wishful thinking? 'I simply need to get fit.'

He gazed tenderly at me for a moment. 'You have nothing to prove to me, Katie.'

'I know, but I'd like to prove it to myself.'

Silence descended between us because I didn't want to speak and break the magical spell woven around us. His smooth voice relaxed me, entered my body and mind, and blocked out everything else.

Could I walk away from this job, from him?

I should. For my own sanity I should run now, but the die was cast. I couldn't leave him now. The Frank Sinatra's song, I've Got You Under My Skin, I heard Mum sing while she peeled potatoes at the kitchen sink came into my head. I sang the words in my head, the meaning of them clear to me. Liam was definitely under my skin.

I sighed, acknowledging my fate. It was true. Liam Kennedy had walked into my life and sent me spinning when all I wanted was employment.

I was to be miserable again for some time it seemed. Only this time, the joke was on me. I was the one lusting after my boss and not the other way around. If it wasn't so tragic, I would have laughed.

Chapter Eleven

Back at the stables, we helped to unsaddle the horses and rub them down. I found the exercise extremely soothing. I listened to the light-hearted banter around the yard, the clip clop of the hooves striking the concrete. I studied the owner and the lovely way she had with people and animals alike. For a second, a tiny moment in time, I envied her and her life. She appeared happy with her lot, secure in her place in life, and I suddenly knew a sense of not having the same feeling. It's possible she's quite miserable and hated her life, but I didn't sense it. When she patted a horse or talked with a rider, the contentment was in her face. She oozed serenity in her manner, and I wished I could have the same.

Until this week I thought myself happy, well happy-ish. Yet, coming up here has shown me that I simply existed and have not been truly living. In December, I would be twenty-nine. One year off thirty. One year! How did the time go by so fast? Things had to change.

I had to change. I *wanted* to change.

Nothing drastic, off course, I wasn't about to cut my hair and dye it purple, or travel to some third world country and work for the Red Cross, or trek the North Pole, or become a vegan.

No, I was simply going to be an adult and sort my life out. I needed to stop pratting about with guys that had 'loser' written in invisible ink on their foreheads. I needed to save money, stop drinking so much, lose a bit of weight, and maybe go back to collage or something and study photography again. And perhaps, just perhaps, some gorgeous hunk of a guy will fall crazily in love with me and buy me a large diamond ring and…and a summerhouse in the Lake District.

Naturally, with those thoughts buzzing in my head, I looked for Liam, but couldn't see him for horses' rumps, and none of them were white chargers.

There I go romanticising again.

With a sigh, I gave myself a mental shake. I didn't want to ruin the day.

I could have easily stayed longer at the stables, only I knew there would be emails to read and phone calls to make when we returned to the hotel. I gave Flossie a pat on the neck and a rub on the nose, then said goodbye to everyone and joined Liam, who'd been talking to the guide.

He smiled at me and we headed for the Land Rover. 'What did you think? Did you enjoy the morning?'

'It was one of the best mornings I've had.' There was no denying it.

Liam gave me a long look, emotions playing on his face. 'A lot different from your London life though.'

'Yes, of course. The only horses in London belong

to the police and the queen, or those crazy people who ride in Hyde Park with all the pedestrians and bicycles and traffic. No, thank you.'

He chuckled. 'The novelty for the country hasn't worn off yet?'

'A novelty?' I pondered his words. 'I don't think of it as a novelty. A change, definitely, but a good change.'

'I bet you're missing the nightlife. You've been in your room each night for a week. I'm sure you're ready to go partying with your friends.'

'At home I don't go out every night, just on the weekends.'

'Every weekend?'

'Nearly.' Did that make me a bad person?

'Don't you grow tired of it?'

'No. It's fun, a laugh.' I shrugged, bewildered. 'Besides, there's nothing else to do.'

A puzzled expression flittered across his face. 'London is full of things to do.'

'Oh, I've done all the galleries and museums. I've seen everything there is to see in London.'

He pressed the unlock button on his keys and we climbed in the car. 'Don't you ever get out of the city and try something new?'

'There doesn't seem the time.' What was with all the questions?

'Do you get drunk every Friday and Saturday night and sleep all day Sunday?'

How did he know my life?

And why did I feel guilty? Isn't that what all single people did?

Only, the way he said it sounded ugly. And I *felt* ugly for not doing other things. I'd got into a rut. No wonder I was bored and unhappy.

Before I could reply, Liam's mobile rang, and I turned to watch him answer it. His face grew serious while talking.

Something was wrong.

I waited until he finished the call and put his mobile in the middle console. 'Has something happened?'

He ran his hand over his head, his sunglasses hiding his eyes from me. 'My grandmother has taken a turn for the worse. Mum said she had another stroke early this morning, a mild one, and she's awake and talking now, but frail. The doctor says she'll recover, but Mum thinks I should come home in case...'

'Oh, Liam. I'm sorry.'

'Thanks.'

'We always feel so useless at times like this, don't we?'

'Yep, it's not good. I'm hoping Mum is overdramatising things, something she does at times, and it's not as bad as she says.'

'Even if it isn't as bad as first thought, you must go home and see your gran and spend time with her.'

He nodded and snapped on his seatbelt. 'I hate the thought of her not being well and that I can't do anything to help her. She's always so active and alert.'

'Hopefully it won't be too bad, and she'll recover and be allowed home soon.'

He reversed and then drove down the drive to the road. 'I can't imagine not having her in my life. She's a brilliant grandmother, always there for people. And such a character. Really smart. As kids my brother and I couldn't get anything past her. She always knew what we were up to.' He paused, deep in thought. 'She'd better recover.'

'I'm sure she will.' He really loved his grandma. My heart went out to him. Impulsively, I covered his hand with mine. His warm skin sent a shiver through me, but I pushed tried not to think about it. As much as I was attracted to him, now wasn't the time to dwell on what could never be. 'We'll be positive.' I gently squeezed his hand and then let go and became business-like. 'Let's go back to the hotel and pack. I'll ring Karen and let her know what we're doing.'

'We'll have to cancel everything for the next week or two, as well as contact the curlers and apologise, reschedule, and— '

'I'll do all that, don't worry.'

He nodded. 'We'll clear the diary for the next two weeks. Afterwards, we'll take it from there.'

'Yes. I'll get it sorted. You've got numerous articles that are finished and proofed. They can be used, buying you time.'

He gave me a sad smile. 'Sorry about this.'

'Don't be silly. There's nothing to be sorry for. This is my job.'

'The good thing for you is that you can go back to London. I don't know for how long I'll be down south, at least two weeks.'

'Right.' I swallowed the knot of misery in my throat and withdrew my hand from his. I didn't want to go back to London. I didn't want to be apart from him. Oh God, this was a nightmare. Why did I have to fall for him, of all people? I might as well as wished for frigging Johnny Depp!

The drive back to Wetheral was nothing like the morning's trip. I stared out the window, feeling totally wretched, and the radio seemed to play every sad love song known to man. What is it with that? Whenever you're feeling down, the DJs wanted to rub it in your face with repeated depressing songs? After twenty minutes of gloomy lyrics of unrequited love, I was suicidal.

Once at the hotel I couldn't find the words to lighten the situation, and instead headed to my room to make the call to Karen, while Liam went to his to pack.

Twenty minutes later, after a mad dash of packing, I answered a knock on my door. Liam had showered and shaved and was now wearing jeans and a dark grey shirt. He stood there, dejected, a bleakness in his eyes, holding his large carry-all. I simply wanted to hug him to me and hold him tight.

'Did you get a hold of Karen?' His tone matched his gloomy face.

I opened the door wider for him to come in. 'Yes, I did. She expected it, having talked to your father. He's in Cornwall, and she's running everything single-handedly like some office Boudicca.'

'Ah, of course.' He looked around my room. 'Will you be all right driving back to London?'

'Yep, no problems.' I smiled to hide my misery. I knew I had to leave but I didn't want to. I had this odd feeling that once we said goodbye today, I'd never see him again.

'I'll ring you when I get to Cornwall, and we can discuss what's happening when I know more about Gran.'

'Okay.' I fought the urge to reach up and caress his check. I wanted to feel his skin, his hair, taste his lips… Every part of me ached to have him touch me, ease the pain in my heart. I wanted to give him some form of comfort to ease his sorrow, to let him know he wasn't alone, that I cared.

'Drive carefully, won't you?' His smile became

more of a grimace. He hitched his overnight bag up his shoulder higher and swapped his laptop case to his other hand.

'I will. You, too. Try not to worry too much about your gran. Call me anytime.' Was he as edgy as I was? Did he hate the thought of saying goodbye too? Likely I was being fanciful as usual. Wishful thinking indeed.

He suddenly grabbed my hand and squeezed it. I didn't know if it was to reassure me or himself. 'I'd best be off then.'

Outwardly calm, I watched him head for the door, but inside I was screaming for him to stop and come back. It didn't matter that he didn't feel that same as I did, I just wanted him near so I could look at him, listen to him, be with him.

'I hate goodbyes.' His ominous words hung in the air between us. Liam opened the door and gave me a dazzling smile that ripped the soul right from my body. 'Be seeing you then.' He winked and left.

Gone.

Just like that.

I ran to my window, but I couldn't see Liam's Land Rover from here. I closed my eyes and let my head bang against the window.

I wanted to cry, but tears refused to come. Emptiness enveloped me. Numb, cold and alone. Those words described me. When would it be my turn to have other, better words to sum me up? Like happy, contented, glowing, fulfilled, loved?

I no longer lusted after my boss, which was bad enough, but oh no, not me, I had to go all the way and fall head over heels *in love* with him!

Brilliant.

My phone rang I grabbed it quickly in case it was

Liam, only Joanna's name flashed on the little screen. I tried not to sound disappointed. 'Hi, Joanna.'

'Hi, how are you doing?'

'I'm good.' I'm shit, but why depress someone else. 'How are you?'

'Fine. Rather great in fact.' Her excitement was barely concealed in her tone. 'Guess what?'

'You got a pay rise?' I checked the car park again for Liam but didn't see him.

'No, though that would be nice.'

I sighed, not wanting to hear a chirpy voice in my ear. There's nothing worse than when you're feeling depressed there's someone bouncy in your ear. That would be outlawed if I ruled the world. But then, if I ruled the world I'd never be depressed because I would be in bed with Liam licking ice cream off his gorgeous chest.

'Come on, guess again.'

I scanned the car park one more time. 'Um…you bought a great pair of shoes in a sale?'

'No, but again, that would be nice.'

'Well, tell me then.' I wasn't in the mood for twenty questions. I left the window and sat on the bed.

'I said yes to Lachlan. We're getting married!'

It took a few seconds for the shock to subside, and then an awful hollow feeling took its place. I couldn't breathe for tears choking me.

'Katie? You there?'

'Yes, I'm here. I'm so happy for you.' And I was, really, I was, but I felt lost too. Abandoned. So much change in such a small time was giving me head spins.

'You're shocked, aren't you?'

'Yes, I suppose I am a bit. After what you said last

128

week.'

'I know. Me too. I never thought I'd say yes. But all this week I've thought of nothing else. I've talked with Lachlan, and he says nothing will change. He doesn't want me to suddenly stay home and have five kids or forget my career.'

'That's generous of him.' God, what a bitch I was being.

'Oh, don't be like that, Katie. I do love him and our life together and well…I realised that if we parted over this then I'd have lost something good. Men like him aren't thick on the ground, you know. You always said I was a lucky cow to get him.'

'True.' I picked at the blanket folded at the end of the bed.

'And I'm not getting any younger. I'm thirty next year.'

'What does it matter how old you are? Don't do it because thirty is looming, Joanna.'

'I'm not that stupid, Katie. I love Lachlan.'

'Are you sure he's the one though to marry? Do you really want this, want him, for the rest of your life?'

'I don't know about the rest of my life. I can't predict the future and people change, but right now I want this and him. He loves me and I love him. It just took me a while to really understand what love was.'

Shame filled me. Here I was making my best friend doubt herself over something that she wanted, and would be good for her, just because I was fed-up. I needed to stop feeling sorry for myself. Taking a deep breath, I gave myself a mental upper cut. 'I want you to be happy, Jo. I love you and only want the best for you. And I know Lachlan is wonderful and decent.'

'Yes, he is.'

'You're going to have a super life together.'

'So, you're happy for me?' I heard the uncertainty in her voice.

What a bitch I was.

'Absolutely delighted.' I injected happiness and love into my voice. 'It's the best news I've heard in ages.'

'I knew you'd be excited.' The relief in her tone was evident.

'You can tell me all about it tomorrow.'

'Tomorrow?'

'I'm coming home.'

'Why? Have you quit?'

'No.' Though I would if I was sensible. 'Liam's grandmother is ill, and he's left for Cornwall, so he said for me to go home until he needs me.'

'But won't he need you down there?'

'Apparently not.' Admitting to it made me feel worse.

I could have gone with him, helped him in some way. I'd have liked him with me if it had been the other way around. Evidently, he didn't think the same as me. I wasn't important enough to accompany him home, to share such a difficult time. Damn, I needed to calm down and slow down. Just because I was in love with him didn't mean he returned those emotions. In fact, I knew he didn't. Why should he? I'm his employee, and we've known each other for a week. Silly really.

'Are you leaving today or in the morning?'

'I'll be on the road shortly. I'll be home late, but that's okay.' I grabbed my bag and finished packing one handed. The room was closing in on me and I had to get out.

'Do you want me to go around to the flat and open some windows and buy you some milk?'

'No, don't bother, thanks. The flat will be fine, I'm sure. I've only been gone a short time. I'll get a few things on my way when I stop for petrol.' Six days. It sounded so little, but to me, it seemed like six months.

Could you fall in love with someone in six days? Was it possible?

'You'll drive carefully, won't you?'

'Yes, of course.' I smiled because Liam had said the same thing to me.

'I'll call around tomorrow then.'

'Lovely.' I straightened from being bent over the bed, collecting up files from earlier. 'Oh, Jo?'

'Yes?'

'I'm very, very happy for you and Lachlan. You'll tell him congrats from me, won't you?'

'Yes, I will. Thanks. I feel better now I've spoken to you. Hugs.'

'Hugs. Bye.'

I continued gathering up my things, packing and sorting, desperately trying not to think of Liam, of Joanna walking down the aisle, or of anything at all but the drive home.

Home.

The thought of returning to an empty flat didn't excite me.

On impulse I rang Mum. I'd stay there tonight. I was in need of Mum's warm embrace and to have Dad chat with me over a cup of tea, while we ate Mum's freshly baked cake. She always baked a cake if she knew someone was coming. I needed their unselfish love to take my mind off Liam and my silly heart that refused to behave.

Chapter Twelve

'So, you're not eating much, lost weight, as miserable as sin, and have no interest in going out?' Joanna stared at me over the rim of her teacup.

'Sounds about right.' I agreed. We were sitting on the deck outside in the back garden of Mum and Dad's place. My staying the one night and turned into two weeks. Two whole weeks of waiting for Liam to ring me. He had once. The Monday following us leaving Cumbria. A short phone call to say he'd be staying in Cornwall for a couple of weeks and he'd not be working on stuff for the magazine for a week or so until his grandmother was over the worst. He said he'd ring me again to let me know what his plans were.

Therefore, unable to bear the solitude of my flat and endless days moping around waiting for Liam to call, I've stayed with Mum and Dad, slept in my old bed and felt totally…dejected.

'I don't think I've seen you so cut up about a fellow before.' Joanna sniffed as though she smelt something bad. 'Why did you have to fall in love with him, for God's sake? It sounds like a really respectable job.'

'I know!' I gave her a defensive glare. 'I didn't plan on it, you know.' I pulled my legs up and put my feet on the chair, resting my chin on my knees. Life sucked. Being in love sucked even more when the one you desired didn't feel the same about you.

'Have you heard from him today?'

'No. I don't expect to.' It could be days or even another week before he rang again. Everything was up in the air. Sighing, I looked down the garden to the huge birch trees at the bottom. Beyond them, the Thames flowed silently past on its way to the city. Mum and Dad were out on it now, in Dad's little boat.

Likely they wanted a day without having to look at my miserable face.

In truth, they'd been very loving and supportive. I had driven home from Cumbria with the radio on so loud it drowned out all thought. When I arrived home, it was late, and I had a magnificent headache. After a cup of tea and a bacon sandwich Mum made for me, I went straight to bed. Then, I spent the next morning reading the paper, washing the breakfast dishes, and talking to Dad until Joanna called by. I had to keep busy to stop thinking about Liam. That weekend went by in a mind-numbing, depressing haze of disappointment when he didn't call. Instead, he had sent a text asking if I got home all right. Texting is so unromantic, but then, he wasn't thinking of romance, was he?

Joanna and the girls had called frequently, begging me to go out, but I decided not to. I wasn't in the mood to have fun. I wanted to wallow. Not very mature, I know, but I believed it to be understandable in the circumstances. Mum must have sensed something wasn't right with me as she kept me busy, cleaning, gardening, visiting Grandma and relatives, shopping, the whole works, plus she cooked wonderful meals. She even bought chocolate chip ice cream and allowed me to eat it straight out of the tub. She was rather cluey, was my mum.

Joanna chose a cookie from the packet we'd brought out to the table. 'What are you going to do?'

'I don't know. Get another job and forget him.'

'Why?'

I frowned at her. 'Why? What do you mean why?'

'Well, why leave a perfectly decent job. I wouldn't. I'd tough it out. You might find in a few months you don't really like him that much.'

Not like him? She was insane. I'd spent six days from morning to night with the guy and found nothing to not like.

Joanna put her cup down on the wooden garden table, and munching on her cookie, sat back in her chair. 'There is another solution.'

'Oh? What? Kill myself?'

'Don't be dramatic.' She brushed some crumbs off her long lemon-coloured skirt. 'You could always sleep with him, you know, become his girlfriend.'

'Yes, you're right.' I gave her a look full of attitude. 'I could simply knock on his door and calmly say, 'Liam, here's some paperwork for you, and oh by the way, I'm hot for you and would like to jump your bones, how about it?''

She gave me a smart-ass smirk. 'Well, not so crudely, obviously.'

'It's no use. He's my boss. I can't work for him and I can't sleep with him.'

'Why. Lots of people do it. Businessmen have

their secretaries as mistresses all the time. It happens. You know it happens, look at Plunkett. Do you honestly think he's the only boss who wants to sleep with his employee?'

'No, of course not.'

'It's common place. Office affairs happen because people are stuck together day in, day out.'

'Have you had an affair with your boss?'

'Yes.'

My mouth fell open in astonishment. 'Really? Why haven't you told me?'

'I did. Remember Carl?'

I thought back over the years. 'Carl…'

'When we first moved in together. My first job in London.'

'Oh yes, I remember.' I scowled. 'I didn't think you slept with him, I thought it was just flirty stuff.'

'It was mainly, but we did have sex on one occasion. It was awful, groping in one of the women's toilet cubicles.' She titled her nose in the air. 'Not one of my most memorable decisions, I have to say.'

'You never stop surprising me.' I grinned and shook my head. 'Besides,' I waved a dismissive hand at her, 'it's more than just sleeping with him. I want to be with him, not only in bed, but all the time. I like his company. And I think he knows I *like* him. It's so embarrassing.' Stupid tears welled, and I looked away.

Damn. Bugger. Shit.

Joanna reached over and grasped my hand. 'I'm sorry you're upset. Are you sure he's worth all this?'

'Yes.' A tear trickled over my lashes and ran down my face. 'I've fallen in love with him, Jo, and I can't have him.'

'What is it with you and men? Lord, you do know how to pick them, Katie. Can't you fall for someone normal? Not a dickhead or a boss? It really isn't that hard, you know.' She hugged me, and I cried on her shoulder until the pain lessened a little.

I leaned back in my chair and sniffled. 'I needed that, thanks.'

'Everyone needs a good cry every now and then.'

'I'm pathetic.'

'Don't be silly.'

'Back in a sec.' I ran inside to grab a Kleenex and dried my eyes. How ridiculous, crying like this over a man who didn't want me. I needed to get a life. Taking a deep breath, I went back outside and sat down, giving Joanna a weak smile.

'Better?'

'Yes.'

'Good.' Joanna took my hands. 'Now I have something important to ask.'

'Oh?'

'I've been waiting for the right moment, but you've been fed-up for two weeks and would've probably said no, so I'm just going to ask. Will you be my chief bridesmaid? Is that what it's called?'

I gave her a mock angry stare. 'I'd have been insulted if you'd asked anyone else!' We hugged and laughed, gushing like we were silly teenagers.

'Thanks, Katie.' Joanna leaned back in her chair; relief evident in her manner. 'I'm so happy that's sorted. If you'd said no, I'd not bothered having a chief bridesmaid at all.' She screwed up her face. 'Is it called that?'

'I don't care what it's called, I can't wait for it all to happen. It'll be so wonderful.' And it would give me something else to think about.

'And expensive.'

'Big or little wedding?'

'Medium, I'm thinking. Lachlan has a thousand bloody cousins and aunts and uncles. They make my side look ludicrous. I'll have about ten, and he'll have a hundred. His mum is going crazy and already I can tell there's going to be trouble with her sticking her nose into everything.'

I remembered Lachlan's mother from a dinner party Joanna once had. The woman never stopped talking and her husband was the opposite and never spoke at all. 'Well, if she gets out of control, threaten to elope. It might slow her down.'

'Nothing slows her down. She's a bloody bulldozer.'

'Will you invite your dad?' I didn't like mentioning her dad, a touchy subject, but it had to be out in the open. Dads usually did the big job of giving the bride away, and I had the feeling that Joanna's wedding might be different on that score.

'No.' Joanna ate another cookie.

I didn't push the subject. After Joanna's mother died when she was sixteen, her dad became a father from hell and virtually threw her out so he could have the house to himself. Joanna lived with her grandparents for a few years until she moved to London and shared a flat with me, Steph, and some other girls.

'Who will walk you down the aisle then?'

'There won't be an aisle. I told Lachlan I want to marry in a park or some lovely big hotel.' She smiled, her face becoming all dreamy. 'There'll be just you and me walking down the carpet.'

'Sounds lovely.'

'It will be; I'll make sure of that. We can discuss it

later though, as I have nothing properly planned yet and need to talk to Lachlan.' Joanna stood and collected our teacups. 'Shall I make us another, or should we go to your dad's local and have a wine?'

'No, I don't want to drink. If I start, I'll not stop and then I'll be even more depressed.' I suddenly remembered the photos I had taken at Cumbria. 'Do you want to see a couple of the photos I took while away?'

'Sure.'

She sat back down, while I ran into my room to grab the photos.

'Here,' I gave her the pile.

'You said a couple.' She laughed, picking up the thick wedge of photos.

'I couldn't help myself. I realised how much I miss photography.'

'You always take great photos. I'll get you to take some of the wedding, too, though Lachlan has a friend who does weddings, and he's promised him the job without even discussing it with me. I tell you this wedding will either make us or break us.' She flipped through the photos of the Lake District and then paused as she came to one of Liam on the mountain. 'This is Liam?'

I nodded, my throat tightening as I gazed at his photo. Boy, did I miss him.

'I'd like to see one without his sunglasses on.'

'But you can see how lovely he is though, can't you?'

'Well yes, but a man's eyes can say so much.'

Inspiration struck. 'Wait a minute, he's in one of the issues of the magazine I have. He gave me some to read, kind of like homework or research.' I raced back inside and searched through my folders and paperwork until I found a few copies of Adrenalin Rush Sports.

Joanna sighed when I shoved the magazines at her. But like a good friend she put up with my fanatical inclinations and opened to the page that had Post-it Notes sticking out.

'Tell me he isn't gorgeous.' I craned over her shoulder to sigh in rapture of a photo of Liam on a fishing boat holding up a huge fish he'd just caught.

'I won't lie, he is attractive.'

'Do me a favour! Attractive?' I huffed and flopped onto a chair. 'Attractive isn't a good enough word for him. He is sublimely magnificent.'

She laughed and shook her head. 'What you like, hey?'

'Admit he's hot, I won't tell anyone, especially not Lachlan.' I took the magazine from her.

Joanna snatched the magazine back and studied Liam again. Then she picked up the photo I'd taken of him and gazed at that too. 'To be honest he seems…'

'What?'

She shrugged. 'I don't know…'

'What?' I frowned at her. 'What does he seem? Gay? Up himself? A loser?'

'Don't get shitty with me.'

'Well, make sense then.' Geez, she knew how to wind me up.

'I'm sure he's genuinely nice in a controlled sort of way.'

'What the hell is that supposed to mean?' I snatched the magazine back and stared at Liam. What did Joanna see that I didn't? Controlled? She talked shit.

'Don't get me wrong, I don't mean to be a bitch,

but he seems like he'd go for someone different than you or me, someone really wealthy, upper class. You know, the whole polo playing set.'

She got all that from a frigging fishing photo? I threw the magazine on the table. 'Don't be stupid. How can you think that from looking at his photo?'

'It's just not the photo but from what you've told me. Really, Katie, think about it. He's wealthy and travels the world. We're talking playboy material.'

'It's his job!' How dare Joanna sum him up so disparagingly? She knew nothing about him.

But then, did I?

Piss it!

Joanna pulled her hair back with her hands and gave me a look of sympathy. 'Let's forget I spoke.'

'It's what you think though.' A heavy weight rested on my chest. 'Controlled. Polo playing set. In another words, you think him out of my league.'

'Yes, perhaps…But there's nothing wrong with that. Who'd want to be like them stuffy people who couldn't have a good time if they tried.'

'He's not like that, honestly. He's down to earth. He's not a millionaire, you know. Rather, just ordinary.'

'Hardly that, Katie.' She frowned. 'He has some money and travels the world, that's not normal everyday Joe, is it? Even your job isn't normal. You've worked for one week and now are being paid to sit on your backside for a fortnight. Who gets that in their job?'

'Well, I know, but—'

'Look, I'm not always right, am I? Don't be upset. Go on your gut instinct, it's the best way.'

I nodded, but misery descended once more to keep me company.

Joanna sighed in frustration. 'Do you see him sitting out on this deck talking to your dad, sharing a beer?'

Actually, I did see that quite easily. 'Yes, definitely. I think he and Dad would get on well. And mum would love him to death.'

'Then that answers that question then, doesn't it?'

'Only the likelihood of it ever happening is-is like me being on the front cover of Vogue, nude and draped in diamonds.'

Joanna stared at me. 'You don't seriously want to do that do you?'

'God no. Well, not the nude bit obviously.'

'You're mad.'

'And sad.'

'Listen, let's hit the shops. No more moping around. I can't stand it.' Joanna jumped up and took my hand, pulling me up. 'We need retail therapy and lots of it.'

I picked up the cookie packet. Shopping? The idea appealed a little. I could buy something nice, a new top or a pair of jeans. I'd lost weight without even trying to. I should trademark it as the non-diet and call it, *The Unrequited Love Diet*. Chuckling, I followed her inside. 'Shopping sounds good. I'd like to get my hair cut too. I might ring Steph and see if she can fit me in.'

Joanna's eyes widened in excitement. 'Then we'll go have dinner somewhere glamorous and afterwards go dancing. Yes?'

'I don't know.'

'It's Saturday night and you've been cooped up here for weeks thinking of nothing but Liam bloody Kennedy. It's time to let your hair down, have some fun. You know I hate it when women change to suit their current boyfriend.'

'That's hardly the case here.'

'Well then, stop acting like he's going to walk through that door any minute.'

I gave in reluctantly. 'Yes, okay.'

'Actually, let's ring the girls, and we'll invite Steph, make a night of it. Steph's always good for a laugh.'

True, my sister had a wicked sense of humour. It made up for her awful taste in men. 'Right, ring the girls and tell them we'll meet somewhere for dinner this evening.'

'Woohoo!' Joanna waved her arms in the air and did a little dance. 'Watch out London, Katie's back in town.'

'I'm not getting drunk, Joanna, or doing anything stupid,' I warned.

'There's a new place that's opened up which plays all the old disco hits. We'll go there and just dance all night. No guys, I promise.'

'That's fine, but I'm not drinking.' I scribbled a note down for Mum and Dad telling them my plans, grabbed my bag, slipped on some sandals and then followed Joanna out to her little sports car. Shopping, dinner, and dancing. Could a girl ask for more?

This girl could, but I won't, at least not tonight anyway.

* * * *

What was it about dancing that makes it so good? I think it was a combination of good music, a dark room and colourful flashing lights, which allowed a person to melt into the beat and not have to worry about a thing. It didn't matter if you couldn't dance very well or if you were fat or thin, pretty or ugly, you were hidden within a cocoon of rhythmic sound

142

and flattering lights. It was the best and safest way to forget one's problems. And tonight, I wanted to forget a lot of things.

Tonight, I just wanted to dance. I kept saying it to Joanna until she told me to shut up as I was sounding like an extra in that Footloose movie.

The beat of a Bee Gees number made me nearly lose control as I danced with Joanna. Steph joined us, and as she grabbed my hands, we twisted and sang loudly. The next song kept me on the dance floor, and the next. The DJ put on *Nutbush City Limits*, and we all lined up to do the moves like we did when we were girls at school. I had to laugh as Steph turned the wrong way and faced me instead of the other way. It was good to spend time with her. I made a mental note to do it more often. Over dinner she'd mentioned that she'd missed me and then tore strips off me for not filling her in about Liam and the new job. I promised to keep her informed from now on as long as she didn't gossip my news to all her clients, a bad habit she had.

After *Nutbush*, another song came on that got us grooving again. Some random guy came up to me, and we did five seconds of dirty dancing before he moved onto another girl. Steph made a lewd gesture about his tight backside, but I twirled away ignoring it. I did not even want to flirt tonight. I just wanted to dance—there, I had said it again. Besides, none of them stacked up against Liam.

God, I sounded pathetic even to myself.

One night. Could I not think about him for one night?

Obviously not.

Maybe an hour then?

One hour without one thought about Liam. I

glanced at my watch. 10:35. Okay, no thoughts about a certain man until 11:35.

I left the girls and went back to our table to grab my bag. I needed to not only pee but to freshen up a bit. The warm airless room did nothing for my new haircut. When I left Steph's salon this afternoon, my sleek short cut looked sassy yet easy to manage. I'd opted for a change. The shoulder length hair had been replaced with layers, the longest length ending at my jaw line. I'd not had it so short for years, but I liked it. Steph had done a superb job, and Joanna and the girls crowed its merits, lifting my spirits. The cut and blonde highlights rejuvenated my appearance, making me feel less a tragic wannabe teenager, holding on to adolescence. Thirty was looming, and I wasn't going to ignore my age, instead I planned to meet it head on and enjoy it.

I pushed my way through the crowded club and made for the ladies' toilets. I'd been dancing for an hour straight and if I didn't go to the loo soon, I'd pee myself. A queue snaked out of the ladies and I joined it, cursing that I left it so long. I bobbed to the music, *Knock on Wood*, a classic eighties song, to take my mind off my bladder. A few guys standing around drinking gave me a come-on smile, but I looked away. Boys. They were such boys after Liam.

Shit. I didn't even make it five minutes, never mind an hour. There was no help for me.

I glanced back at the dance floor and spotted Joanna, Steph and Fiona dancing. The other girls were guarding our table. We took it in turns to dance so we'd always have a table to keep our bags, hold our drinks and to collapse at. Though, I wasn't drinking, at least not alcohol. Just dancing. The music was good—all old disco songs people could bop to and none of that head-banging stuff that made your ears bleed. From the moment we entered the club, I hit the floor and hated coming off it. Hence, my over-full bladder.

The queue inched forward and for a second I wished I were a man. There were never any queues to men's toilets. Funny that.

A woman staggered into me, smiled and apologised, and then promptly fell over. She lay on the carpet, her skirt up to her waist, flashing her green panties, laughing her head off until her friend pulled her to her feet again. Loudly swearing and cackling like hens, they swayed away together. For the first time ever, I realised how unattractive it was to see women so completely drunk they'd lost all dignity.

I'd been living like that for years. My stomach churned at the notion. No more. Never again would I go back to that life. There had to be something more that getting razed every weekend and going to work on Mondays with a sore head. I knew there was more, for I'd glimpsed it that week with Liam. I wanted someone to share my life with, someone who made me laugh and made me think.

What was I going to do?

The queue inched forward again and at the same time my mobile rang in my bag, a smaller bag I changed to for tonight. The little screen on my mobile lit up with Liam's name and my heart stopped for a fraction before it started banging like drummer on speed somewhere in my throat. 'Hello?'

'Katie?'

I could barely hear him for the music, but it didn't matter. He had rung me, and that simple action was like winning the lottery. He hadn't forgotten me. 'Yes, it's me.'

'It's Liam.'

Of course, it is, you glorious creature, you! 'How are you?'

'I'm good. Sorry to be calling so late. I only just realised the time and by then you'd answered.'

'I don't mind.'

'Pardon?'

I left the queue and moved closer to the bar, hoping it would be a little quieter and easier to hear, but it wasn't. 'I said, you can call me any time.' I sounded such a desperate loser.

'I can barely hear you. What's that noise?'

'Music.'

'Are you having a night out?'

'Yes, with some friends.'

'Oh, okay. Sorry I disturbed you. I'll ring you tomorrow. Bye.' The phone went dead in my ear before I had the chance to reply.

Guilt, thick as syrup, filled me. I don't know why. Perhaps it was because he was visiting a sick grandmother? No, that wasn't why. To be honest with myself, I did know the reason. I felt guilty because he'd think I'd forgotten him and the week spent in the country and returned to my old life, which I had, well kind of. It was ridiculous to feel this way, I mean, I wasn't answerable to Liam. But he didn't know that even though I was at a nightclub, I wasn't really being the old Katie. The old Katie had gone somewhere, and I was rather glad about it too. She was becoming boring. And of course, I only came out *to* forget him, but he didn't know that either. I couldn't believe he had to ring tonight, of all nights. Why hadn't he rung during the week when I'd been home on Mum's bed watching Steel Magnolias and crying into four thousand Kleenexes, or when I'd been mowing the lawn because Dad's back was playing up again? Oh no, he didn't ring then. He had to ring when I was out at a nightclub, which would only confirm his thoughts about me that I was some sad thing that had to get drunk every weekend.

Oh God, I was turning into some tortured creature of self-doubt.

Sodding hell.

What was going through his mind right now? Likely, he thought I was having a wonderful time, doing my thing, but in reality, I was miserable and fed-up, and it was all *his* fault. I could have managed to keep living my life as it was.

No, that wasn't true. Under all that drinking and partying I was unhappy, only I didn't know it until now.

Substance. I had no substance to my life; it was true.

Hark, listen to me. I'm doing bloody psychiatry on myself now.

'Katie. What are you doing?' Steph, her long blonde extension swaying as she bounded up to me near the bar, purse in hand, ready to buy more drinks for everyone. 'What do you want to drink?'

'Nothing, thanks. I'm going home.'

'Home?' Her eyes, the same hazel colour as mine, looked worried.

'Yes, I've had enough.'

'But it's still early.' She left the bar and came closer, a look of concern on her face. 'Are you sick?'

'No, just tired.'

'You haven't been yourself all night. I've never known you to be so quiet. Are you sure you're not coming down with something?'

'Positive.'

'I talked to Mum earlier and she and dad are worried about you too. They said you've changed after returning from Cumbria. What's upset you? I saw you talking on the phone just then. Who was it? Has your boss turned into another bastard?'

'No. No, absolutely not, really.'

'Well, what's happened? You're not being normal. Oh God. Are you pregnant?'

'No!' I laughed at the horrified expression on her face. 'I'm definitely not pregnant. You need to have sex for that. Look, I'm fine. Honest.' Even as I spoke the words, traitorous tears threatened.

'Tell me.'

'It's nothing.' I kissed her cheek, and she hugged me tight. Despite her tendency to be a bit loopy at times, she was a darling.

'Ring me if you need me.'

'I will. Say good night to the others for me.' I escaped into the crush of people and made it outside. Three women were climbing out of a black cab and I quickly jumped in when they were clear and gave the cabbie directions for my flat as it was closer than my parents' home.

I think this is the first time I've ever been the first one to leave a nightclub out of our group.

Bugger.

Chapter Thirteen

Banging on the door woke me. I raised my head and blinked. I was on the sofa in the lounge room and not in my bed. The banging continued. What the hell? Was there a bleeding fire?

Sleepily, I untangled myself from blankets and pillows and stepped to the door, unlocked it and opened it. Through blurred vision I made out Joanna. 'Morning.'

She raised one eyebrow. 'So, you got home okay then.'

I frowned and padded to the kitchen sink, yawning. 'Why wouldn't I?'

'Well, you left without saying goodbye. You would have snapped my head off if I'd done that to you.'

For a moment I had no idea what she was talking about, then remembered last night. 'Sorry, I was tired and didn't want to ruin everyone's night. I thought it best to come home.'

'I would have left with you.' She scowled at the blankets and pillows on the sofa. 'Did you sleep in here last night?'

I yawned again and filled the kettle. 'Yes. I was watching a movie and got comfy. It didn't end until late, and I couldn't be bothered getting into a cold bed.'

'I thought you were tired, but you watched a movie?'

'I think I was too tired to sleep. You know how it is. Overtired.'

'I don't like seeing you like this.'

'Like what?' I brought two cups out of a cupboard and yawned again. It'd been about four in the morning when I last looked at the clock. Sleep wasn't happening for me lately.

'With no spark. You didn't eat much dinner last night, you left the club early, and you're up all night watching movies, not sleeping.'

'I'll be fine.' I was getting sick of saying that. 'Did you dance until dawn?' Though she didn't look weary or hung over. She looked smart like she always did. Even in casual weekend clothes she always looked well groomed.

'No, we all left not long after you. I was in bed for midnight.'

'Oh dear. I'm a bad influence, aren't I?' I laughed.

'I'd had enough anyway.'

I spooned sugar into the cups and then turned to Joanna. 'Make some tea for us while I go to the loo.'

My mobile rang as I headed to the bathroom. I ran to get it, and my stomach clenched when I saw Liam's name light up. 'Hello?'

'Hi, it's Liam. I didn't wake you, did I?'

'No, not at all.' I beamed over at Joanna, who shook her head at me. I was a lost cause, and we both knew it.

'Sorry to be phoning on a Sunday.'

'It's not a problem. How's everything going?'

'Gran's doing much better, though still frail. The doctors are happy at her recovery so far.'

'Oh, that is good news.'

'Yes. Um…I was wondering if you'd mind coming down to Cornwall. We can work down here.'

My heart seemed to swell to the size of a football in my chest. 'Sure. When do you want me?'

'Can you come down this weekend?'

'Yes, of course.'

'I don't want to leave the area until Gran is back to normal. I thought we could work from Cornwall for a couple of weeks. I don't expect we'll be doing too much though. It'll be part time mostly, but the weather is good, so you can consider it as a holiday, too, if you want.'

'I'll come down today.' I looked at the clock on the bookshelf. 9:21 am.

'Are you sure? I don't want to interrupt your plans.'

'I don't have any.' Why lie and pretend I was busy? I wasn't into playing games. He needed me, and I wanted to be with him. True, our goals were different but that didn't concern me for the moment. I just wanted to be where he was. Never in my life had I acted this way about a man before, but I couldn't help it. Would I ever be cured?

'Are you going to drive or take the train? If you take the train, I can drive you back.'

Decision made. 'I'll go by train.'

'Can you ring me when you get to Liskeard? I'll collect you from there, which will save you changing trains to Looe.'

'Okay, thanks.'

'Are you happy to stay at Gran's house or do you want a hotel?'

'I don't mind staying at your Gran's, if there's room.'

'There'll only be Mum and I staying there. Dad's heading back to London and Gary's off to Thailand now Gran is doing much better. Gran's house is a decent size. There's room.'

'Okay, well, I'll pack and catch the first train I can to Cornwall.'

'See you soon.'

'Bye.' I hung up and smiled at Joanna. 'I'm off to Cornwall.'

'I gathered that, and going by train, amazing.'

'Well, it isn't the tube.' Happiness gripped me like some tropical fever. 'I'll be staying with the family, too, in the grandmother's house. I'll meet Liam's mum.' I couldn't keep the nervous excitement out of my voice.

Joanna carried in two cups of tea and passed me mine. 'Be careful, Katie. Try to not fall any deeper in love with him if you can help it.'

'I think it's too late for that.'

'The more time you spend with him, the worse it will be when you leave.'

'I know.' Of course, I knew, but it couldn't be helped.

'Why didn't you tell him that you quit? It'd have been far easier to do it now than later.'

'Because I can't.'

'Oh, Katie.' She sighed and sat down. 'This is going to end badly; I can see it. He's hardly rung you in the last two weeks, what does that tell you?'

I shrugged, not wanting to admit to the truth yet. 'I thought all night about him, Joanna, and I can't walk away.'

'You're going to be miserable, or I should say, continue to be miserable.'

'I'd rather be miserable with him than without him.'

'It's not as easy as that, and you know it.'

'I'll see sense one day, no doubt. Just be ready to help deal with the mess I'll be in when that time comes.' I shivered. Feeling as I did now, I knew why I'd gone so long without falling in love. Being upset and emotional one minute and hysterically happy the next did my head in.

'Don't go, Katie. Ring him back and say you can't. Give him any old reason. Do you want me to do it? I'll ring him. Honestly, you'll get over him quicker if you quit now.'

'No. I'm going.'

'You'll only get hurt.'

'Then I'm a sucker for pain.' I paused in taking a sip of tea. 'I can understand why there are so many pitiful love songs now. I have joined the ranks of the *unloved*. I think I lived in a bubble before I met Liam.'

'For heaven's sake, stop being a drama queen. Everyone falls in and out of love all the time, you're not the only person, you know. And you're making him out to be some saint, for God's sake. He's a man, like all other men in the world.'

I glared at her. 'Why are you in such a foul mood?'

'Because I feel like you're changing.' She sighed. 'Everything is bloody changing.'

'It happens. We grow up. Make decisions.'

'I just don't want to see you unhappy. I wish to hell I'd never told you about that interview.'

I thought of my interview with Karen. It seemed ages ago now. A turning point in my life. No matter the outcome, I'd never regret it. That day had changed my life. 'Maybe when I get down there, I'll be able to tell him that it's not working out.' That would confuse him, as he gave me the impression he liked how well we worked together as a team.

'Yer, right. I doubt that. You're too starry eyed about him.'

'I can't help it. We spent a whole week together and we talked and laughed. Liam taught me things, showed me that there was a world outside of London.'

'Oh, shut up, you're talking shit.' Joanna sighed. 'Stop talking as though you're some virginal mouse who's never had fun. We've travelled and—'

'I know! I didn't mean it like that.' I slumped back against the sofa. I couldn't explain my feelings. My heart told me that Liam was *The One* and since this was the first time *The One* had ever showed up in my life, I wasn't behaving normally.

'I'll go and leave you to pack.' Joanna stood and took her cup back to the sink.

The tension crackled between us. We both knew things were changing, and it had us off kilter. For so long it'd been just the two of us, with Lachlan skimming the outskirts, but now, the dynamics had changed. Joanna would be getting married and Lachlan would always come first, and I had changed not only jobs, but my outlook. What I previously had, how I lived my life no longer seemed enough.

'I'll take care of your mail again.' Joanna came back and hugged me. 'Ring me during the week and let me know how you're getting on.'

'I will. Thanks.' I kissed her cheek. We were

friends again. 'I know you want the best for me, as I do for you.'

She smiled and all was forgiven. 'I'll have the chocolate ice cream on standby for when you come to your senses.'

'Okay but allow me a few more weeks of drooling pleasure before I become rational again and leave him. I need some memories to keep me going when I'm old and wrinkly.'

'Well, remember you've got chief bridesmaid duties to look forward to. So, all is not lost.'

'As long as I'm not wearing pink lace,' I warned.

'Pink lace and ribbons in your hair!'

'Or worse, those flower circlets that make you look like Jesus' daughter.'

She laughed and headed for the door.

Once she left, I quickly rang Mum and asked if it was all right to leave my car with them and told them of my plans. Next, I packed and booked a cab. Then I showered and changed, taking a great deal of care about my appearance. Wearing black jeans, a white blouse and my hair washed and shining, I added a touch of makeup and was pleased with the result. Weeks of not eating much, and hardly no crap food, plus minimal alcohol, and the fresh air of Cumbria had altered me some. I noticed my eyes were clearer, my face less puffy and my waistbands looser. Another couple of weeks of this, and I would be a lot closer to my goal weight too. Being miserable and in love did have its benefits.

Cornwall, here I come!

Chapter Fourteen

I stepped off the train and walked along the Liskeard station platform. Ahead stood waiting and I smiled, doing my best to ignore my knee-knocking reaction and concentrated on not dropping my bags or laptop. I couldn't believe how thrilled I was to see him again. It was rather pathetic. I expect to be excited, but my heart lurched at the sight of him and I wanted to run into his arms and hold him tight. I wanted to smile and laugh and get everyone's attention so they could see that this attractive man was waiting for me. They wouldn't know that the relationship wasn't platonic. They'd think we were lovers, maybe even husband and wife…

Oh Lord, I shouldn't have come. My fantasies were already getting away from me and I'd only this minute arrived. How would I go staying in the same house as him?

Take a deep breath, Katie.

When Liam got closer, he took my bag from me. 'You made it then.'

'Yes.' If I'd had a free hand, I'd have checked my

hair again, although for the last ten minutes in the train I'd done nothing but make myself look the best I could.

He studied my hair. 'You've had your hair cut. I like it.'

'Thanks.' Relief ebbed out of me like a slow tide. He liked it. All was right in the world!

'Sorry about my clothes. I've been gardening at Gran's and I thought I'd be finished before you texted me.'

'I made good time.' Naturally I refrained from mentioning the hurrying I did from the time he called to arriving at the train station. I'm sure I set some world record in the short time it took. The taxi came on time; the train was waiting to pull out of the station when I got there, and it had no delays while on route. Everything had gone to plan.

Once at his Land Rover, I took the opportunity to give him the once over while he stowed away my luggage in the back. He wore old faded jeans, in places covered with streaks of dirt, and a dark t-shirt that had a few drops of paint on it. He hadn't shaved today, and stubble grew, making him look so damn sexy. The clean, working apparel of Cumbria had given way to dusty gardening clothes and for some insane reason I fancied him even more when he was scruffy. The urge to rip his clothes off and kiss every inch of him flooded through me like a monsoon.

I jumped into the car and fiddled with my seatbelt, knowing my cheeks were flaming. If I was going to survive this week in Cornwall, I needed to stop fantasising about him. Sadly, it was going to be easier said than done.

'All set?' Liam asked, starting the engine.

'Yes. How's your Gran doing?' I strove for

normality.

'Doing really well considering.'

'That's such good news.'

'She's sitting up, eating, and talking. Her left side is a little weak, but she's coping and adjusting.'

'That's from the first stroke? Did she have two or was it something else?'

'Yes, two strokes. The first one was the worst. The second one, when we were in Cumbria, was much milder thankfully.' He paused as he waited for a car to pass and then turned out onto the road. 'They were worried she wouldn't pull through the first one, and then to receive another so soon after sent everyone panicking, thinking it was the end, but she's tough old thing.'

'She sounds wonderful.'

'She is. We're hoping they'll let her go home sometime this week. That's why Mum's staying down here, well that and to also sort out the paperwork for the hotel they've bought.'

'I hope your mum doesn't mind me staying at the house? I can go to a hotel if need be.'

He glanced at me and flashed a wry smile. 'It's fine, there's room enough. Gran's house is big. Though if you stay at the house you'll be expected to wash up and stuff. No standing on ceremony.' He winked, and I melted. I would have dug tunnels to China if asked.

We were passing beautiful countryside, and, as we went over a rise, I glimpsed the ocean in the distance. Since meeting Liam my perception of things had become clearer. I don't know why, but they were. Colours were deeper, aromas more invigorating, sounds more stimulating.

Soon we were turning down into a narrow lane and

as Liam steered the vehicle, I watched his hands on the wheel. He had long tapered fingers, lovely hands for a male.

'Gran's house is in West Looe, but not in town. It's on the coastline, the best property in all of Cornwall.' Liam grinned. 'Not that I'm biased or anything.'

'No, of course not.' I laughed, liking the warmth and friendliness that we'd slipped back into as though the last two torrid weeks hadn't existed. I suddenly wanted us to be good friends, naturally lovers, too, but it was important we become firm friends. To not have him in my life seemed wrong. I instinctively knew that I could rely on him, no matter what, and that thought gave me such tremendous pleasure and a feeling of security. And, as weird as it sounds, I believed I wasn't alone anymore.

'Gran's property runs to the edge of the shoreline, so we have access to the beach. It's only a small beach and unusable when the tides are high, but as kids, Gary and I loved coming here every summer. I want my kids to share the same experience.'

'You want kinds?' I asked, my breath held.

'A couple, yes. Do you?'

'Yes, I do.'

'You are getting ready to settle down then?'

'I think I have been for a while, but no one has come along.'

'You've been filling in time.'

'Maybe…I suppose so, yes.' Christ, I sounded such a desperate loner. 'I'm not saying I've been a crying wreck, pining for some knight to rescue me.'

'I didn't think that for a minute.' Liam grinned. 'I think you've been having the time of your life. A real London party girl.'

I smiled but didn't know how to respond and so remained silent.

He turned onto a drive and through an open gate that had a sign proclaiming the place to be *Wanderer's End*. I liked the name instantly. The driveway rounded a short bend and then the house, painted white with a grey slate roof, loomed before us nestled against a backdrop of tall trees.

'This is it.' Liam stopped the car at the side of the house in front of a double garage.

'What a lovely house.' I climbed out and helped with my luggage before we walked around to the front. I gazed at an unstructured cottage garden framed a wide lawn. Through the gaps in the trees and bushes I noticed large open fields beyond. 'No thatched roof?'

'No. This house never did have thatch.'

The red front door opened and a tall woman, wearing dark slacks and a cream blouse walked towards us, smiling. 'Here you are then. Welcome. Lovely to have you here. I'm Meghan.' She stopped and kissed both my cheeks. Her smile was sincere, and the warmth in her eyes relaxed me immediately. 'You must be Katie, who Liam's told us so much about.'

'Yes. Thank you for having me. I don't want to be any trouble though,' I prattled, shocked that Liam had mentioned me to his family. What had he said?

'Nonsense, no trouble at all. You're very welcome. I told Liam it made sense to have you here. This old house needs people in it.' Meghan, who, with clean, unwrinkled skin and a modern hairstyle, didn't look her age, guided me inside and in the entry hall I paused to gaze around, liking the period features of beams and stonework.

Meghan turned to Liam. 'Take Katie upstairs and show her where she'll be sleeping and let her freshen up. I'll put the kettle on.'

Liam sighed and shook his head at his mother's retreating back. 'She rules us all. Come on, I'll show you around.'

I followed him up the staircase, across the wide landing and down a hallway to the last bedroom on the right.

'This is one of the guest rooms, and Gran's best room. So feel privileged and special.' He chuckled, dumping my luggage on the double bed.

'I do, thank you.' I surveyed the lovely room, tastefully decorated in colours of light green and cream, with touches of gold here and there. Along the wall was a small dresser and teak drawers. I stepped to the closest window, which held a cushioned window seat overlooking the back garden and the fields beyond. Standing on tiptoes, I could just see over some of the shorter trees to the sea in the distance. 'What a fantastic view.'

I glanced a Liam who came to join me at the window. My skin tingled at his closeness, I could smell his cologne, a different one this time to the one he used in Cumbria. If only I could touch him, kiss his lips and feel his arms around me. The bed behind us was very tempting…

Wishful thinking.

He turned to look at me and I gazed back, wallowing in the opportunity to simply stare. 'Thanks for coming down, Katie.'

'No need to thank me. I wanted to, and it is my job.'

'I'm not sure how much work we'll get done. To be honest with you I shouldn't have asked you to come, and I'm not sure why I did.' He frowned. 'Mum visits the hospital every day and we all decided Gran's house needed a tidy up before she returns home, and that's been left to me. So, you see, there won't be much magazine work being done, but Mum thought it would be a clever idea to have you down here in case something came up.'

'I'll help you with the house then, when we're not working for the magazine.' I shrugged. I didn't care what I did as long as Liam was nearby. I liked the fact he'd asked me to come here even though the possibility of working wasn't high. Did he want my company too, as I wanted his?

Don't get ahead of yourself, Katie girl.

'You're not serious?' He looked sceptical. 'You can't be happy to help clean and garden around here? That is certainly not part of your job.'

'I don't care about that.'

'We'll pay you.'

I took a step back, offended. 'Don't you dare. Being down here is like having a holiday. It's so beautiful, it'll be a pleasure to help about the place for my bed and board.' I smiled, hoping he'd see I was earnest.

'Thanks. You must think us slightly odd, but foremost we are a family business. I doubt many businesses have their staff staying in their family home.'

'Maybe we can be friends as well as a working relationship. Would that be so bad?'

'No, not bad, but…' He hesitated; his expression serious.

'Let us see how it goes, yes?' I injected brightness into my tone to the lighten conversation and to steer it away from dangerous issues. 'Is the bathroom across the hall?'

He gazed at me for a moment and then turned for the door. 'Yes, I'll show you.'

After I'd been to the bathroom and freshened up, Liam showed me the other bedrooms and then we went downstairs and peeked in at the comfy sitting room and dining room just as Meghan called the tea was ready.

'Mum has baked a cake, I think, or bought one at least.'

'Great. I'm starving.' I followed him down the hallway to the kitchen at the back of the house. The kitchen was a huge room, a real country kitchen with wooden dressers, a large table and a shiny green Aga. It was one of the best kitchens I'd seen.

Meghan mashed the tea and had it all set out on trays. 'I thought we'd have it outside under the tress. It's a beautiful day. Liam can you carry this tray out and check the table for bird deposits, please? There's a little brush in the tray.'

I stood back and gloried in watching the mighty man being told what to do by his delightful mum. I took the next tray holding the cake and cookies and Meghan showed me where to go—through the spacious and airy conservatory and out into the back garden, which sloped a little down to the trees. Beneath a large oak, Liam was brushing the table.

The day was warm and summery with just a hint of a breeze in the top branches of the trees. Perfect.

'Liam tells us that you enjoyed horse riding, Katie.' Meghan smiled, pouring out the tea.

'She's a natural.' Liam winked at me. He cut the sultana cake, put a piece on a plate, and passed it to me.

'We used to have a couple of horses in the fields

behind the house that the boys' rode. But we sold them when my husband's father died. Gran didn't need the responsibility of looking after them when we weren't here. Plus, the boys became busy, too, and couldn't always come down here to exercise them.'

I looked at Liam. 'No wonder you were so good at it. You grew up with horses.'

He shrugged with devilment in his eyes and bit into his cake.

'I adored the horse riding and want to do it more often. The Lake District is beautiful, especially from a mountain top.' I laughed at Liam. 'But seeing it from the back of a horse is a unique experience for me, and not as strenuous as hiking.' I took the teacup from Meghan. Did I sound gushy?

'Liam told us he tortured you with that hike. That's wasn't so kind of him.' She gave him a stern look. 'We are enormously grateful that Liam has an assistant who is willing to try new things. It makes working together so much easier.'

I glanced down at my cake. She had no idea what lengths I'd go to in trying new things with Liam. Inside I laughed at myself. What an idiot I was, drooling over this woman's son like some rock band's groupie. Where was my sense of pride?

Gone.

Oh well. I'll not worry about that now.

'Liam, you should show Katie around town this afternoon. There's plenty to see.' She turned to me. 'Have you been to Looe before, Katie?'

'I don't think so. We used to have lots of holidays when I was little and I know we've come to Devon and Cornwall before, but not sure if we went to Looe.'

'It's a lovely place. Busy in the summer, but we

mustn't complain about that as there's a lot of local businesses who depend on the tourists.' She turned back to Liam. 'Take Katie this afternoon.'

'What's with all the orders?' He raised his eyebrows at his mother.

'An afternoon off won't hurt.'

'I am taking the afternoon off from the magazine. I was going to get on with the gardening.'

'You've been gardening all morning.'

'And not even half done.' Liam drank the rest of his tea and stood. 'I want to burn off all those weeds and rubbish down the back.'

'You'll do no such thing while we have a guest who is here on her first day,' Meghan said with a raise of her eyebrows. 'I would take Katie myself, but you know I have things to do.'

'Mum, I—'

'No, don't argue. It's a beautiful afternoon. Take Katie and show her the harbour. The gardening can wait until tomorrow. Besides, it's Sunday. So, relax for once, will you? You've worked on one thing or another the whole time you've been here. You need to learn when to slow down.'

'Don't feel you have to take me anywhere, Liam,' I butted in. 'I'm happy to stay here and help you.' The last thing I wanted to be was a nuisance.

Liam glanced at me, his aggrieved expression revealing more than words. 'No, we'll go. Anything to shut Mum up.' He smiled at me to show he was only joking, but the look he gave his mother held a touch of annoyance.

I grinned. His mother was wonderful.

Within ten minutes we were back in the Land Rover heading for Looe. Liam had washed and changed into casual shorts and a black t-shirt, again looking so damn gorgeous. I forced myself not to stare at him, at the way his short pulled across his muscled arms. Again, I wanted to kiss him right there and then until neither of us could breathe.

Once in Looe we were lucky enough to find a parking space near the waterfront. The great weather had driven hordes of tourists to the area. The sounds of happy kids competed with traffic noise, seagulls and shoppers.

'Fancy an ice cream?' Liam asked, as we walked down the street.

'Love one, thanks.'

While Liam went to buy ice creams, I visited a few shops. I bought some cheap funny souvenirs for the girls, a Looe tea towel for Mum and a wind chime for Steph as she loved the things. Personally, I thought they were a right pain in the backside. I couldn't find anything for Dad, but I had time later to search for something. Leaving the shops, I spotted Liam gazing at the boats, licking his ice cream and holding one for me.

'Thanks.' I took mine from him and licked it.

'They'll melt in no time.' He grimaced as his began to drip. 'I don't know why I buy them, they're so damn messy.'

'That's half the fun.' With my tongue I scooped up a bit that was in danger falling off the cone. I noticed Liam watching intently, and a secret thrill went up my spine. Did he find me a little attractive? Just a tiny weeny bit?

'Want to walk down to the end of the pier?'

'Okay.' We fell into step, not talking much, simply enjoying the weather, the scenery. The tide was in, and the fishing boats bobbed and swayed like drunken men on the way home from the pub. There was a slight breeze coming off the water, and I lifted my face to it.

I wished I could take Liam's hand as we walked, but that would have freaked him out. Maybe I should do it anyway? Joanna could be right; he might be too controlled. No, I didn't think he was. He seemed to be quite balanced and normal. It was me who was the freak.

Instead of taking Liam's hand as I longed to do, I brought my camera out of my bag and took some photos of the harbour, the boats and shops. I even managed to get another one of Liam when he wasn't looking. More memories captured to keep me happy in my old age. At this rate I'd be a lonely old pensioner with no family to spoil just photos to cry over.

I was such a sad git. No wonder he didn't fancy me.

Chapter Fifteen

The next morning, I woke early. Surprisingly I'd slept well, despite the torturous knowledge of having Liam sleeping across the hall. I stretched out in the comfortable double bed and thought of the night before. After coming back from Looe, where we spent a couple of hours walking around, I helped Meghan cook dinner, a small roast beef with all the trimmings. We'd eaten it in the kitchen and the three of us had talked for hours about anything and everything. Liam was coerced into doing the washing up since we cooked, though I did dry up for him just so I could stay in his company.

Afterwards, we refilled our wine glasses and headed into the sitting room where we sat on the large sofa and talked some more, although we were meant to be watching a movie. I can't even remember the title of it, which shows just how interesting I found it.

I yawned and stretched again, smiling at nothing. Whipping back the covers, I hung my legs over the side of the bed. I felt dreamy and idle. I'd spent most of yesterday with Liam doing nothing much at all and loved every second of it. Today promised another day of being the same. What a decadent way to live.

I washed and dressed, putting on a flowing white skirt and a pale pink shirt. Liam had mentioned about going for a drive into Devon to research some sports enjoyed by the southern counties. He also wanted to interview a few of the surfers in North Devon. My watched showed the time at 6:40. It didn't feel that early. Usually if I saw that time at home, I'd throw the covers over my head for at least another half hour.

Brushing my hair, I gazed out of the window. It was a beautiful August day, and the trees were alive with birds singing and hopping about. I liked waking up to this. It won hands down over screeching tires and horns blaring which is all I got from my flat window. I wondered how I lived my life as I did before. It seemed so rigid, so dull. Was I a secret country child? First Cumbria and now Cornwall. Did I have the call of the wild in me?

I chuckled and dabbed on some make-up. I'd always thought I had the call of the *devil* in me.

Maybe I wasn't the self-absorb party girl I thought I was.

I stared at the mascara brush without really seeing it. If my old life was no longer me, then what did that leave?

Stuff it. The day was too beautiful to self-analyse.

I threw the mascara back into the toiletry bag and headed downstairs for breakfast. In the hall I stopped to admire the framed family photos lining the walls. I smiled at the photo of a young Liam and Gary holding puppies and another one of them on a tyre swing. Liam was a beautiful child, as was Gary, but my gaze kept straying to the photos of Liam. Even as a boy he had eyes that looked into the camera as though he was smiling just for you and sharing some great secret.

I wanted a son like him.

As the thought popped into my head I straightened, alarmed. Marriage, children? What was happening to me? I seemed to be thinking of nothing else lately. Was my biological clock winding up, beginning ticking loud and clear?

In the kitchen, Meghan cooked bacon and eggs while listening to the local radio station. I smiled warmly at her, hoping to show her how comfortable I was here and how much I liked her. I would have liked her even if she wasn't Liam's mother, but that she was, made it all the better. 'Good morning.'

'Good morning, Katie. How did you sleep?'

'Like a baby.'

'Oh, good.' Meghan flipped on the toaster. She was smartly dressed in a duck egg blue skirt suit. She was an elegant woman, her hair and makeup perfect, but for all that, she was happy to wear a flowery apron around her waist and cook a fry-up. Now that was classy. Popping the baked beans on to warm, she glanced over at me. 'You'll have breakfast, won't you? I've cooked enough for an army. A terrible habit of mine.'

'Yes, thank you. I never miss breakfast.' Though sometimes it's been a McDonald's breakfast when I was running late, but she didn't need to know that. 'What can I do to help?'

Meghan passed me the plates. 'Set those on the table, will you, love? And can you get the juice out of the fridge?'

I set the table, the bacon aroma making my stomach growl. I could never be a vegetarian. One sniff of bacon and I was a goner.

'Do you enjoy cooking?' I asked, wanting to learn more about her.

Meghan placed paper napkins on the table. 'Yes, though I'm not terribly good at everything and stick to the old favourites, but I do enjoy it now. I didn't when the boys were young. I hated the monotony of it.' She added salt and pepper shakers to the table. 'What about you? Do you like cooking?'

'I don't mind it, but I'm not very clever at it. I need to take a few courses to be better.'

'Actually, they have some wonderful weekend cookery courses in Paris. I read about them in one of the magazines. Wouldn't that be fun, Paris and food and shopping? Maybe we should go one time and then I can come home and teach the chef at the hotel something new.' She laughed at her own joke. 'To be honest, now we have the hotel I'm hoping I can just eat at the hotel's restaurant all the time.'

'Well, there has to be some perks, surely,' I said, cheekily. 'I know that's what I'd be doing if I owned a hotel.'

'Yes, it's going to be a huge change for us, but a good change, I think. I never expected to be in the country full time, but Clive needs to retire from the magazine. He's worked hard for so long. Our retirement was meant to be our time to slow down, but what do we do? We buy a hotel.' She laughed and shook her head. 'We must be mad.'

The toast popped and I buttered it on the bench. Sunshine streamed through the window, lighting up the kitchen and reflecting off the silver service displayed in a tall dresser on the far wall. This was a lived-in kitchen. In fact, the whole house had a warm comfy feeling about. No wonder Liam got pleasure from his summers here as a child. Every child should experience a house like this in their childhood.

'Liam's gone to the shop for me.' Meghan turned the stove off and carried the plates of bacon, sausage and eggs to the table. 'He said for us to start without him.'

'I wouldn't have minded waiting.' I sat down and poured orange juice into Meghan's glass and then my own.

'I have his warming in the oven. He'll be along shortly.' She dished out the food and we started eating. 'Tell me all about yourself. You have family?'

'Yes, parents and one sister.'

'And you're close to them?'

'Oh, yes. I don't have any woeful tales of my parents not being there for me, thankfully. They raised my sister and me in a loving home. We were lucky.'

'True. Not everyone has a content home life, which is distressing. We Kennedys are the same as your family, all very close.' Meghan added a dash of salt to her egg. 'And you live in London?'

'Yes, that's right.' I cut my sausage.

'London is a young people's place I think.'

I chewed my food. 'I agree, but I don't see myself as living there forever.'

'How are you finding working with Liam so far?'

Quickly swallowing a mouthful of egg, I took a sip of juice. 'I'm finding it remarkably interesting.'

'Good.' Meghan left the table and switched the kettle on. 'Liam works too hard. Try and get him to slow down if you can. I'd really appreciate it.'

I watched her set out the teacups, wondering why she said that. 'Yes, of course. At least, I'll try.'

'He's too much like his father, all work and no relaxation. He'll become ill…' She sat back down and cut her bacon. 'His sports help him to unwind a little, but I don't think he's enjoying the work as much as he did. Something is not right with him. He's restless. I'm not sure how he'll be when he's in the London office full time. He was never one to be cooped up indoors.'

I paused in eating to concentrate on what she was saying. I felt her unease and her eyes, so like Liam's, looked worried. She was talking as though I was a part of the family not an employee. Taking a sip of juice, I waited for her to say more, hoping she would.

'You know Gary doesn't have an assistant?'

'He doesn't?' Frowning, I cut some more sausage, but my appetite had suddenly vanished. What was she telling me? My skin goose bumped. Was she hinting that Liam didn't need one too?

'No, he doesn't. Gary can handle all his work by himself. True, he's not as proficient as Liam and spends his time surfing around the world when he could be writing more articles, but that's Gary. He's a law unto himself. Clive and Liam think he's lazy, but he's just more laid back then they are.' She shrugged one shoulder in a carefree way as though she had long accepted Gary for what he was. 'Liam doesn't really need an assistant either, or he didn't want one after Alison left, but we all convinced him that he should.' Meghan glanced at the back door as though expecting Liam to walk through any minute. 'We thought if he had an assistant he might, well, slow down a bit and his workload would be eased a little.'

'I see.' Did I? I wasn't sure what she wanted me to say. I didn't even know what to think. Breakfast wasn't going as I imagined. Why weren't we talking about the weather? This was so personal I squirmed in my seat.

'I'm only telling you this because you'll be working so closely with Liam. He'd be very annoyed to hear me talk like this, but I'm sure you can keep this to yourself.'

I nodded; breakfast forgotten. I felt like a conspirator yet couldn't help myself. I had to know what was going on. She obviously wanted to talk and unburden. Only, it seemed disloyal to me to talk about Liam this way.

'You see, Gary knows how to relax, how to enjoy himself while working. He doesn't care about deadlines and all that nonsense. He drives his father crazy, he's so laidback. However, Liam is the total opposite, always has been. Gary's easy going, a risk taker. While Liam is sensible and reliable, too much at times. Sometimes he's strung as tight as a coil.'

Oh God, Joanna had been spot on about Liam. Clever cow. How did she manage to sum him up from a few photos and my comments? Perhaps it was because she worked with similar type men?

'I worry about him. His father says I shouldn't, that Liam's always been a loner, but he's thirty-three in March and needs…oh I don't know what he needs.' She shook head and moved her food around the plate with her fork. 'I shouldn't interfere, I know. Nor should I be talking like this to you. I apologise if I've made you uncomfortable.'

'I'll help all I can, if I can.' What else could I say?

She looked up and smiled. 'Thank you. When I first saw you, I thought to myself that you were the right kind of person to help me—someone decent and honest. I'm typically good at summing people up.'

'How can I help you?' What was she on about? What was I getting into? Me and my bloody big mouth.

'Liam needs bringing out of himself. He doesn't talk to me about it, but I sense he's been unhappy. His health scare frightened us all, but instead of slowing down he's working harder. Why, I don't know. He doesn't need the money. He's done well in that area. I just don't understand him at the moment.' Tears filled her eyes and she wiped them away, smiling. 'Oh, I'm stupid I know. But he's my boy, no matter how old he is, and I hate seeing him working so hard for nothing.'

Health scare? I stared in amazement. He seemed healthy enough. Hc strode up that frigging mountain like a trained athlete. I tried to remember any time he seemed to have looked ill, but nothing came to mind. 'I'll take as much of the work load off him as I can, but he's driven and dedicated and good at what he does. When we were in Cumbria, I noticed how many articles and features he'd done in the last year. A remarkable amount. I emailed articles to America and Canada for him, and they were immediately asking for more.'

'There, you see, he never stops. I don't think he sleeps much. Alison, his former assistant, although very nice, was serious and committed, a high achiever. She and Liam worked well, got so much done, but neither of them knew how to slow down and relax.' Meghan brought the tea to the table and sat down again. 'I was glad she got married and wanted to have children. It gave us the opportunity to find someone new.' His mother sniffed away the build-up of tears. 'Ignore me, I'm stupid and emotional.'

'There's nothing wrong in caring about your son.'

She rose to make some more toast. 'You know, Karen rang me after she had interviewed all the women for the job and said you were the best.'

'Oh? That's lovely.' Should I be relieved to have Miss Karen's seal of approval? I guess I should, after all, she ran the London office like a sergeant major and was obviously close to the family too.

'We had a little secret, you see. I'd told her how worried I was over Liam working too hard. I'll share this with you, as I know you'll not mention it to anyone, and you should know anyway being his assistant. Liam has had high blood pressure problems in the last few months. Gave us all a fright, it did. And you hear of stories all the time about fit young people dropping dead of heart attacks. A year ago, a friend of ours lost her son to a heart attack as he was out jogging. Forty-three he was. Forty-three. Married with a small baby. I don't want that to happen to Liam, not my son. When Liam told me of his blood pressure I nearly passed out, I tell you. Who'd have thought such a fit and healthy man would have such a thing? But he stresses so much about work and everything. He works seven days a week, never takes a holiday to just do nothing. Have you noticed how focused he can be?'

'Yes, a little.' To be honest, I didn't think he was any more uptight than some of the businessmen I knew who had much more demanding responsibilities than Liam, but Meghan was obviously concerned about it. I'd have to pay more attention to him, in a non-drooling way.

'Karen and I, both agreed that he needed an assistant to not only cut his workload down, but someone who'd be the opposite to him. She said that out of all the applicants, you were the only one who was fresh and appealing, not too serious. Perfect for Liam. He needed an assistant who'd make him laugh a bit. That you knew little about sports also helped you get the job because we knew Liam would stop and show you the sports he enjoyed. In effect, you'd slow him down, but be so nice about it, he wouldn't care.'

My heart dropped like a stone. What did they mean? Was I some frigging guinea pig to use to make Liam's life calmer? I thought I got the job on my skills and intelligence, my experience as a P.A.

Apparently not.

I got the job because *Karen* saw me as some scatter-brained chick, who would make Liam laugh. She's seen straight through me at that interview. She'd realised that I wasn't a high achiever, that my attitude about getting the job was a little uncaring. They'd wanted someone who'd do the work, but also know how to enjoy a good wine and put my feet up. Someone to slow Liam down.

Oh my God, and I'd done that. In Cumbria he had put off working on several occasions to take me fishing, hiking and horse riding.

Used. That's how I felt. Used. They had used me to bring down his blood pressure. Such a slap in the face. No wonder he looked at me strangely sometimes. I bet he thought Karen was off her rocker to suggest me as an assistant. I was the opposite to Alison and like no one he'd dealt with before. How bloody marvellous. I was a joke.

Meghan frowned. 'I haven't said too much, have I? You don't mind me confiding in you, do you? You aren't offended in anyway?'

'No.' Another lie.

'I have no one to speak about my worries to really. Clive, my husband, doesn't understand, and Gary is useless in things like this. I can't speak to Gran about my thoughts, as it'll only worry her, and she has enough to be concerned about.' Meghan's anxious tone made me pause in playing with my food. 'I know you haven't been with Liam for long, but you both seem to work well together and make a good team from what he's told me. Of course, Liam would be angry if he knew I'd been meddling, but I'm his mother and it's my job to be worried. It's not as if he has a wife to care for him.'

I forced a smile. Naturally I didn't mind being told I was employed to be a distraction. *Not*.

I stood and took my plate to the sink. All this information made me want to leave. I didn't want to be responsible for making Liam slow down. He wasn't a child for God's sake. He would know his own limitations. Yet, if I went then I'd feel guilty for giving him more work to do.

Why did Meghan have to blurt all that stuff out to me? When I woke up this morning, I felt great, now I didn't know what to think or feel.

The sound of a car on the drive alerted us to Liam being home. I rinsed my plate and glass, waiting for him to come inside. When the back-screen door opened, I turned and looked at him. My heart skipped a beat when he smiled at me, his eyes warm and gentle in greeting.

I knew then that I would stay and work hard to lessen his load.

What else could I do?

I loved him.

Chapter Sixteen

'Sit down, Liam. Your breakfast is being kept warm.' Meghan moved to the oven and took out his piled-up plate.

'I don't want a heap, Mum.' He sat at the table. 'On the radio they forecast rain for the rest of the week.' He looked over at me. 'Would you mind if we stayed here today?'

'Sure.'

He tucked into his breakfast. 'I want to do more in the garden while the weather holds. We can do magazine work in the rain, but I can't clear the garden in it.'

Meghan poured him a cup of tea. 'The doctors think Gran can come home in a few days. She'll be so happy to see how tidy the garden is. You know how independent she is, and she'd never admit that it was all getting too much for her.'

'I'll help you.' I filled the sink with hot soapy water, needing a distraction from watching him eat. There were no words to describe how pathetic I was.

'Really?' Liam looked at me in surprise. 'You don't have to. You could take my car and explore the area if you wanted or read a book, whatever. Do anything you want.'

'No, I want to help you. I like gardening.'

'This will be more about burning rubbish and clearing than actually gardening. Gran never throws anything away, and there's crates and junk everywhere in the bottom shed.'

'Not a problem. Let me do this and then I'll go change and give you a hand.'

'Leave that, Katie, I'll see to it.' Meghan smiled and then turned to Liam. 'The veggie patch needs sorting too. There are vegetables that need picking, and some have gone to seed, which need pulling out. Your Gran was distressing about that the other day. You know how she gets. Hates to see anything wasted.'

'Okay. I'll see to it. Tell her not to worry.'

'She won't stop.' Meghan sighed. 'I'm off to the hospital in half an hour and then afterwards I'm going to the hotel. I'll be gone all day. You'll both see to yourselves for a meal later?'

He nodded. 'We'll sort something out.'

'Take Katie out for a meal. It's the least you can do if she works in the garden all day.'

I helped Meghan clean the kitchen and then I raced upstairs to change into old jeans and a shirt that I'd pushed into my bag on impulse, just in case we went horse riding again, or pig wrestling or motorbike jumping. You'd never know with Liam and that excited me.

The kitchen was empty when I returned downstairs. Once out in the garden, I followed the sound of noise. The garden was long and wide, with various outbuildings, a glasshouse and vegetable gardens. A column of smoke rose behind a small wooden shed, and around the corner of it I found Liam raking clippings, leaves and debris onto the flaming pile. Beside him was a stack of old broken crates, even a three-legged chair.

'What would you like me to do?' I asked, sticking my hands in the back pockets of my jeans.

'Can you rake this lot onto the fire, and I'll get some more?'

'Right.' I took the rake from him and continued the task while he collected more stuff to burn from different areas of the garden.

We worked solidly for an hour before Liam stopped and came to stand next to me. Much of the rubbish had been burnt and the area was much tidier.

'Thanks for this.' Liam had brought down two glasses of cold lemonade and handed me one. 'You didn't have to do garden work here.'

'I'm enjoying it.' That was a slight exaggeration. I was hot, sweaty and smelt of smoke. Definitely not a package of desire I wanted to represent, that's for sure.

'None of it is in your job description though.'

Neither was falling in love with you.

I kept the smile plastered on my face and sipped my drink. 'I'm your assistant, so that's what I'm doing, assisting you.'

'You're a good sport.' He winked at me and then drained his glass. 'Now the vegetables.'

I grinned and followed him to a long narrow patch filled with tomatoes plants growing tall and tied to stakes.

Liam grabbed a bucket from near the tap and handed it to me. 'Can you pick all the ripe ones while I work in the next bed?'

'I think I can manage it.'

'Why Gran has to plant so many things I've no idea. She can't physically eat them all and ends up giving most of it away.'

I glanced over the beds full of plants of cucumber, tomato, onions, lettuce, potatoes, beans, strawberries, mint and parsley, not to mention the small orchard heavy with fruit. I became a little wistful. 'I think it would be very satisfying to grow your own produce. To eat something, you've grown and know it's good for you.'

'Cheaper too.' He paused from walking away, his gaze inquisitive. 'I never took you as someone who'd think like that.'

Frowning, I hitched the bucket under my arm. 'What do you mean?'

'Well, you're a town girl.'

'London isn't in outer space, Liam. I do know where vegetables come from. I know what happens before they are packaged in plastic wrap and stored on supermarket shelves.'

'I didn't mean that.'

'Then what did you mean?'

'It's just…' He ran his hand through his hair, clearly uneasy. 'When I first met you, I took you as someone who wouldn't get her hands dirty. Someone who'd hate to be in the country away from the lattés and shoe shops. A person who lived for gossiping with girlfriends, drinking, partying and all that.'

He had my life down pat. Was I so shallow? Yes. Or at least I had been.

'I'm glad you've proved me wrong.'

I gave a hollow laugh. 'Oh, I wouldn't say you were completely wrong.'

'You've shown me I shouldn't have pigeonholed you as a complete city chick...'

'A city chick without brains. That's what you mean, isn't it?' I knew the words he'd left off that sentence.

'No, I don't mean that at all. I know you're intelligent. I know you have courage and will face challenges.' He stared at me and the air crackled around us. Was it my imagination or did something close to craving flash in his eyes?

'I'd best get on with it.' He stepped back, withdrawing from me again.

I turned away and yanked at the red tomato at eye level. Bugger it! What was wrong with him? Was he gay? Didn't he know how to read signals? Couldn't he see how much I wanted him to kiss me? What did I have to do, beg, or write it in permanent marker on my forehead?

The day grew hotter as we toiled. After a short lunch we managed to work at opposite ends of the garden, and I liked to think we were both lost to our own thoughts about each other. How my imagination ran away with me at times.

I worked constantly, wanting to show Liam I wasn't frightened of physical work and that my nails, which were ruined, didn't bother me in the slightest. Liam kept glancing at me when he thought I wasn't watching. It pleased me to know that I'd surprised him again. I wanted him thinking about me.

We started packing away the garden tools around four o'clock. Storm clouds were gathering on the horizon, though the heat remained. Sweat glistened on Liam's forehead and in places his shirt stuck to him. I hoped he'd take it off.

He kicked some of the ashes closer into the smouldering fire and then looked at me. 'Fancy a swim?'

I swallowed. Swimming meant Liam would be shirtless.

Oh Lord.

I swallowed again and gave him a weak smile, wondering how on earth would I be able to control myself with a half-naked Liam? A fully dressed Liam was hard enough to handle.

'Did you bring a swimming costume?'

'Yes.' I'd packed for every eventuality.

'We might find the tide is against us, but we can have a look. Go change and I'll put out the fire.' He grabbed the garden hose and turned it on to put out the embers.

I wished the fire in me could be put out so easily.

Chapter Seventeen

We stood on top of the cliff watching the ocean waves crashing into the little bay below. The breeze was stronger on top of the cliff but not cold. The setting sun, where it streamed through the gathering clouds, cast a band of gold across the ocean turning it to glimmering bronze and orange.

'It seems like the tide is going out, so we'll have an hour or so of the beach. Ready to go down?' Liam took my towel and slung it over his shoulders, then walked to the beginning of the path that wound its way down the cliff side. 'It's not as bad as it seems. We've made steps in places over the years. It doesn't go straight down either, but kind of zig zags.'

I walked over to stand beside him and looked down at what appeared to be a rocky little goat's track. 'I'm not frightened.' No, but I could bloody break an ankle for certain.

He grinned. 'No, I didn't think you would be.' He took my hand, and I relished the feel of his skin against mine. I held tight and it had nothing to do with being scared.

In fact, as we skidded and stepped our way down, I felt completely alive. Seagulls cried, rising and lowering on the air currents. The salt smell of the sea filled my nose, and, as we jumped the last steps to the blonde sand, the pent-up energy burst inside my chest. I wanted to scream and yell and run around.

Unable to contain myself another moment, I stripped off the summer dress I'd worn over my swimming costume and raced across the warm sand to the water.

'Wait for me,' Liam called, yanking off his shirt.

I didn't turn back. I needed to do something, anything, to release the adrenalin pounding through my body. It was either swim or jump Liam's bones. I preferred the latter but the other person's consent is needed.

I let out a gasp as I plunged into the water. It was cold but not unpleasantly so. I kept going until it was deep enough for me to swim. I swam a few strokes and then screamed when two hands grabbed my waist.

Twisting around, I squealed as Liam came up out of the water. I gripped his shoulders to keep from going under. My breathing grew shallow as I stared into his laughing eyes.

We were so close, only inches separating us. His shoulders and upper arms were well defined and muscled, but not in an over the top, Mr Universe pumped on steroids kind of way. I kneaded his shoulders with my fingertips, wishing I could lick off the saltwater clinging to his skin.

His gaze dropped to my lips and then back up to my eyes. Desire flared in his eyes. His hands tightened on my waist. I leaned forward, aching for him. I wasn't imagining the hunger in him. He did want me as much as I wanted him. For a tantalising second, I thought he wanted to kiss me, too, but then he pulled back, putting some distance between us.

Damn it! Why was he doing this? I couldn't stand it.

'I could have been a shark.' He grinned, shaking the water out of his eyes and releasing me.

'A shark with hands?' I wished his hands were still around my waist, but like him, I pretended it was all a huge joke.

'Or a giant octopus.'

'Or Neptune?' I playfully splashed water at him to cover my frustration. What did it take to get him to kiss me, for heaven's sake, a bloody gold-plated invitation?

He splashed back, nearly drowning me. I pushed at his shoulders, but he grabbed me and dunked me under the water, and I came up spluttering. I launched myself at him trying to sink him, but he easily caught me and dunked me again.

'Enough!' I spluttered, but my laughter died as I realised how close we had become again, and how near his bare chest was. I wanted to run my fingers through the fine sparse hair that grew there. My nipples peaked, and I was thankful the water covered my chest.

Liam's eyes widened and his gazed roamed my face. I couldn't hold back anymore. I was tired of hiding my desires and I let my eyes send him messages my mouth couldn't utter. If I had a chance with Liam, then I wanted to take it and stuff the job. I inched closer, letting my breast brush against his chest. I wanted his touch, his mouth on mine. I wanted him throbbing inside me, whispering my name…

'Let's swim.' He ducked away, striking out for the end of the bay.

Point blank refusal.

There you go, Katie. You offered yourself to him on a platter, and he ignored the temptation. What does that tell you!

Stupid, stupid, stupid.

I slapped the water, closing my eyes against the hurt, which squeezed me like a vice. What possessed me to make the first move again? When I thought about it, he hadn't given me enough of the right signals, had he? Why had I rushed it? For once I wished I used my head before jumping in feet first. How did I get it so wrong?

Now I'd have to go home, quit, go back to Joanna in humiliation and say, you were right, I'm an idiot.

I floated on my back, shutting my eyes against the hot tears that gathered there. What had I done?

Why didn't he kiss me? What did it take to find a decent man to love me?

The water turned cold, or it might have been my own shivers of helplessness, but swimming had lost its appeal and I headed back for the beach.

I grabbed my towel and quickly dried myself and then pulled on my dress. The last thing I wanted was Liam to see my imperfect body. Despite wearing my best bikini, a rich shade of chocolate, I wasn't a size eight and never would be. I'd already made him rejected my advances; I didn't want my unattractiveness to turn him into a monk as well.

Sighing, I sat on the towel, wishing my legs were longer, my hips smaller and… Well shit, I might as well just wish to be Angelina Jolie for what good wishing did.

From under my lashes I could see that Liam was

still swimming. Poor man, he was likely as embarrassed as I was. It must be dreadful to have someone you employ fancy you. I was 'doing a Plunkett' on him.

I spread out my towel more smoothly, laid down and closed my eyes.

How would I face him when he came back?

Shit.

I had two options. Pretend it didn't happen and get on with working together or quit.

Right now, neither seemed tempting. I just wanted to die really. How many times had I said I would quit? A dozen or more. But it seemed cowardly. I was many things, I know, but a coward? Never.

'Are you hungry?'

I opened one eye and watched Liam grab his towel and dry his chest, a bloody hot, smeared-with-honey-lickable chest. I turned my head away. 'Yes, I am a bit.' More lies. Good job I wasn't a Catholic, I'd be in the confessional until they posted me a free senior's bus travel card.

'We'd best go up before the tide changes.'

I stood and gathered my towel and headed for the path without looking at him. I went up first and realised halfway up that he'd had my backside in his face, but I was past caring. At the top I kept walking, aware of him right behind me. I didn't know what to say to break the silence. I needed to say something eventually, but what? Nice weather? Seen any good movies recently? I groaned inwardly. This wasn't a situation I often found myself in, and I had no idea how to deal with it.

Once back at the house, Liam took my towel and dumped them in the utility room. 'Did you want to have a shower first?'

189

'Okay, thanks.' I was desperate to put some distance between us. I hated the tension. My shoulders ached from me being uptight. I needed a few minutes to relax and a hot shower would help.

When do I tell him I am leaving?

After my shower.

'Which would you prefer, dinner out or something easy here tonight?'

A secluded table for two in some restaurant with romantic lighting wouldn't help the situation. I'd likely propose, and this disastrous situation would be complete. 'How about something here? I'm happy to have tea and toast.'

He smiled a slow wry smile. 'I'm sure we can do better than toast.'

'Anything easy will do.' I edged to the doorway wanting to escape. Did he have any clue how one simple smile from him nearly brought me to my knees? I had to stop making a fool of myself. He was like an obsession, which wasn't healthy. In fact, I didn't understand myself now. I wasn't acting normally, but then, I'd grown bored of my old self, so what did that leave? Confusion reigned in me. I didn't know which way to turn or how to make it better.

Once dinner was over, I'd have an early night, and we'd both not have to deal with my unwanted advances. A win-win scenario. By morning I'd be gone.

'How about a salad with something?' Liam walked into the kitchen and opened the fridge. 'There's some pork chops and…' he took out a plate of chicken fillets, 'chicken?'

'Lovely.' I took another step. I'd have agreed to eating sheep testicles if it'd got me away from him quicker.

'I'll get this started then.' His brightness annoyed me.

Why couldn't he see the devastation in my eyes?

'Um, actually…I'm not that hungry after all, and I have a bit of a headache, must be all that sun today.' It was true my head was pounding, but it had nothing to do with the sun. 'Would you mind if I skipped dinner?'

'No, of course not.' Concern clouded his eyes. 'Did you want me to get you some paracetamol?'

'I have some in my bag, thanks.'

'You'll need something to eat.'

'I might have a cup of tea later. I think I'll lie down for a few hours, have an early night.'

'Sure.' He looked hesitant, as though he wanted to help but not sure how.

'Goodnight.' I flew along the hallway and took the stairs two at a time, not very ladylike I grant you, but no one saw me. I just had to get away from him and the atmosphere. If only I could get away from my thoughts and tragic heart as well.

In the shower I allowed myself the indulgence of a few tears of misery. I wanted to sob my heart out all night. But how would I explain the red bloodshot eyes to Liam in the morning?

My mobile rang as I started to dress. When Joanna said hello my chin trembled with more tears welling.

'How's it going?' she asked.

'Oh, fine,' I lied. Lying was becoming second nature now.

'You don't sound fine. What's happened?'

I sighed heavily. 'It's just been one of those days. That's all.'

'In what way?'

'Oh, you know, in the way of falling in love with a

191

gorgeous man who sees you only as his employee. That and the added bonus of his mother telling me I was hired to be a diversion, so to speak, to slow Liam down before he developed an ulcer or had a heart attack. You know how it goes. Fun old Katie to the rescue.'

'Come home, Katie. You're going to make yourself ill.'

'I might just do that. Come home, that is. Anyway,' I gave myself a mental shake, 'how are you?'

'I'm normal. I love a man who knows I *exist*.'

'Thanks for rubbing it in.'

'Well really, Katie. Enough is enough. Make a decision.'

'Yes, I know.' Go or stay. Go or stay. I was like a bloody yo-yo.

'What did they mean you were hired to slow him down? That's sounds unprofessional.'

'It was something Liam's mum and Karen, in the London office, cooked up. No one knows about it. Meghan, his mum, just wanted someone who'd not be as driven as him. Karen interviewed me and said to herself, 'Oh this girl is perfect, she is a P.A. with no career ambition and is a party-goer, just what Liam needs.'

'What shit. How could she tell that from an interview?'

'Who knows, but she did, and I got the job. I did everything they expected. I made Liam take time off to take me hiking, horse-riding and fishing. I did the paperwork, made the phone calls and all the other PA stuff but I never really pushed myself or him. Whereas when Alison worked for him, the pair of them had work booked up a year ahead. She had meetings and interviews lined up for him months in advance.'

'Give yourself a break. You've only been with him a brief time.'

'Yes, and in that time, I didn't give a rat's arse about the working side of it. I was too busy drooling. Let's face it, I'm a lousy personal assistant. I always have been. I don't care about their meetings, posting their mail, picking up their dry cleaning, restaurant bookings or dentist appointments or any of that stuff. It bores me to tears. There, I've admitted it.'

'So, what are you going to do?'

I sighed, feeling like crap. 'I don't know.'

'You need a job that interests you.'

'Agreed.'

'Come home.'

'Yes, I will. In the morning.'

'Promise?'

'Yes. I thought I could handle this, but I can't. It's too hard.'

'Good, you're seeing sense. Okay, well, have a good night and don't worry about it all. Text me when your train gets in and I'll meet you. I'll leave work and we can go have a coffee somewhere.'

'Lovely. Good night.' I hung up and sat on the edge of the bed. Joanna was right. I need something for myself.

A career change.

A life change.

Starting tomorrow.

Chapter Eighteen

The following morning, I rose late, due to the fact I tossed and turned all night and only fell into an exhausted sleep around five in the morning. But the midnight hours had allowed me to do some thinking, way too much thinking to be healthy really, but the end result was I'd hand in my resignation today. As to the future, well, photography played a part, so a few courses would be a step in the right direction.

I showered, dressed and headed downstairs with a determined step. No more balking, being undecided or plain chicken. I wasn't happy working with Liam so I might as well leave and go home and learn to live with it.

The house was quiet and empty. On the kitchen table was a note from Liam.

Katie,
I'm taking Mum to see Gran and then I'm heading to Portsmouth to visit a new deep-sea diving centre.
I've other business to attend to, so I'll probably be

gone all day.
Feel free to use the house as you wish.
I thought you'd enjoy a day to yourself
after all your hard work yesterday.
Liam.

Why didn't he wake me and asked if I wanted to go too?

A day to myself?

What crap was that? Tears surfaced and I blinked them away rapidly just as my mobile rang in my pocket. I looked at the little screen. Karen. Excellent.

'Hello Karen.' I glanced at my watch, quarter past ten.

'Hi, Katie. Listen, have you got ten minutes?'

'Yes.'

'Oh good. I'm up to my ears here and there have been problems all morning with the next issue. Our computers have been down for an hour, driving us all a little crazy. Do you have your files handy?'

'Yes, I have. Give me a minute to get them.' I walked into the lounge room where I'd stored my laptop and briefcase.

'You know, we are all impressed with how well you've settled in with Liam. He's very happy with you.'

I paused in opening the briefcase. 'He is?'

'Absolutely. He told me last week how pleased he was. It's awfully hard being a personal assistant. Not everyone can do it. And in this job, it is doubly hard because of all the travelling and deadlines.'

'So, I've done my job then?' I couldn't hide the sarcasm in my voice.

'Pardon?'

'Well I was employed to slow Liam down because

of his high blood pressure, or so Meghan tells me. A dedicated career achiever wasn't what you were looking for. No wonder I got the job so easily.'

'That's not strictly true, Katie.'

'No?' I slapped the flies on top of the laptop.

'No. Please don't think there was anything underhanded in it.'

'Well it doesn't matter now. I'm resigning.'

'Because of that?' Karen's voice rose an octave. 'You can't be serious.'

'I'm deadly serious. Liam doesn't need a personal assistant. He needs a holiday. He needs to go away somewhere warm and relaxing and do nothing but read books by a pool or something.' I stopped as I heard another talking in the background.

'Sorry, Katie, I have to go for a moment. Can I ring you back?'

'Yep.' I ended the call and sat on the nearest chair. Terrific. I'd behaved like a spoilt child. I shouldn't have taken my unhappiness and frustration out on Karen. With a deep sigh, I slowly stood and went into the hallway. I stared at the photos of Liam and let the tears fall before climbing the staircase feeling like an old woman—a dejected, ugly, useless and unloved old woman.

Upstairs, I started packing. I hope Liam didn't expect me to work out a notice. That would send me completely over the edge.

Tears blurred my vision so much I couldn't see well enough to pack my toiletry bag. In temper and frustration, I threw the lot of it across the room. Bugger it!

I slid to the floor, curled up into a small ball and cried liked the broken-hearted fool I was.

* * * *

A noise woke me. Lifting my head, I listened. Rain. Heavy rain hitting the window. The bedroom had grown dark from the late afternoon weather. I glanced at my watch. Jesus! I'd slept for four hours. Shit.

I scrambled up and quickly gathered my scattered toiletries and jammed them into the bag. Joanna would be expecting me on the train. Damn. How had I let it happen?

'Katie?'

I jerked my head up, looking at the closed bedroom door. Liam. He's back. Double shit.

'Katie?' A knock came at the door. I stared at the handle expecting it to turn.

'Yes?'

'Are you okay?'

'Yes, fine.' My heart raced.

'Have you eaten?'

'No.' When had I last eaten? Yesterday? Yes, yesterday lunch time. Lord. Size eight here I come!

'I haven't either. I thought I might cook us a late lunch or early dinner?'

'Lovely thanks. I'll be down shortly.'

'No problem.'

I sighed and leant against the wall. Why had we talked through a closed door? Talk about barricades around the heart, except I must take it one step further and erect a giant freaking castle complete with a crocodile filled moat. One minute I'm giving him signals so large they are picked up by passing satellites and the next minute I'm hiding behind closed doors. He must think of me as truly bizarre.

In the mirror I caught sight of myself and shuddered. I looked like crap. Pale, lifeless, shadows under my eyes, my clothes rumbled. Hideous.

Like a nutter, I flew around stripping off my clothes searching wildly for something better, brushing my hair and generally acting like a puppet whose strings had been cut.

When I made it downstairs, dinner was underway, and my stomach grumbled at the smell of the chicken cooking. Liam was opening a bottle of white wine.

I needed to tell him I was resigning.

Do it now, Katie.

I spotted the plates and cutlery out on the bench top. 'Shall I set the table?' I offered.

Yes, I'm a coward.

After dinner, definitely after dinner I'd tell him.

'Sure. I thought we'd eat in the conservatory. It has a table and chairs in the corner. They're comfy. We can listen to the rain.'

'That'll be nice.' Could my conversation be any more inane? My startling wit was bound to win him over. *Stop it!* I'm not going to win him over no matter what I do.

'I'll go jump in the shower. I'll be two minutes.'

I carried the plates through. The conservatory was a fantastic room, all white and green, with large ferns and glossy plants on stands. The cream wrought iron table had matching chairs, but the chairs were covered with thick light green cushions. If I owned this house, I'd live most of the time in this room. It overlooked the back garden and again if this had been my house, I'd have planted some roses and a colourful garden to soften the appearance of the sheds and vegetable garden.

What was I doing daydreaming about this house for? Clearly my brain had lost the last sensible cells it had. I think I left them in the sea yesterday. Fish were dining on them right now and commenting to each other that they weren't too filling.

I chuckled at my ridiculous thoughts. Yep, it was official, I was insane.

I needed to leave here and Liam if I wanted to retain any sanity.

'Here's the salad.' I straightened as Liam came in, freshly showered, and placed the salad bowl in the middle of the table. It looked wonderful, crisp lettuce, tomatoes, red peppers and cucumber. 'There's small potatoes ready, too, and the chicken is nearly done.'

I smiled, not trusting myself to speak. He wore khaki linen cargo trousers and a pale cream shirt and looked like he's just stepped out of a men's fashion catalogue. Did he unconsciously make himself look so freaking hot just to torment me?

Finding it difficult to breath, I went back into the kitchen and brought out the rest of the table settings while Liam drained the potatoes and placed the chicken on a plate. It was all very homey, and it made my heart ache even more.

Joanna was right. This was too much. I was being dumb thinking I could pull this off. What processed me to believe I could be normal with Liam, when every ounce of me wanted to be in his arms? I wanted him, not just a one-night stand, but a deep and intense relationship.

We sat down and filled our plates. Dinner smelled superb. So, Liam could cook too. His talent list was endless. I was beginning to hate him.

'I hope it's okay. I'm not the best cook.' He smiled, pouring us both some wine.

Anything more elaborate than a cheese sandwich was good in my book. 'I'm sure it'll be lovely. Do you cook much?' If he says he's trained with some famous French chef, I'll throw my wine at him.

'Not often at all. I live off whatever is on a hotel menu mostly.'

'Like we did in Cumbria.'

'Yes.' He smiled and I felt the connection between us spring to life again. 'But I liked to try my hand at cooking when I'm down here. Well, when Gran gets out of the kitchen long enough to let me. She teaches me a little and it gives me a chance to do something for her, but she is such an excellent cook that I prefer her meals to mine.'

'So, Gordon Ramsey can sleep at night knowing you're not after his job?'

He laughed and added dressing to his salad. 'Yes, he's very safe. I couldn't stand cooking in a restaurant. Way too much responsibility.'

A cut my food and ate it slowly, wracking my slow mind for something intelligent to say. Poor Liam was doing his best to act normal and put the beach episode and my hasty retreat last night behind us. Though the evil part of me wished he'd not be such a gentleman and take me up on my offer. If I was going to leave, and really, I must, then a hot night of passion would be a great memory to take with me.

Liam sipped his wine. 'I was talking to dad last week and he mentioned that with Gran being ill, he and mum are changing their plans and coming down here to live earlier than expected. He will retire from the magazine within the next two months.'

'That's a big decision.' I sipped my wine, waiting for him to continue. I liked how he told me things. He didn't have to mention his family's plans to me, but that he did made me all warm and gooey.

'Which means Gary and I will jointly be running the magazine. It also means that the current way I've been living will change.'

Was he hinting I was out of a job? This would save me from thinking of a decent excuse to tell him why I quit. Still, the idea of not being connected to Liam in any way in the future hurt. Christ, what was wrong with me? It was impossible for me to make a decision, and even harder for me to stick with it once made. I never used to be so scatter-brained surely?

Honestly, all this falling in love business was simply crazy.

After this episode with Liam, I was staying clear from love. I'm sure being a spinster could be just as enjoyable. I could end up being one of those old women you see living in a villa in Portugal with deep brown tans on their crinkly skin, wearing huge straw hats and white linen pant suits. The kind that form British citizen clubs in foreign places, so you spend your days speaking with people, who back home you'd not even bother waving to if they were your neighbours.

I could do that.

Liam cut a piece of chicken fillet. 'I rang Gary this morning, and we had a long chat. He's not keen on being at the London office yet, at least not for a couple of years. He likes the tropics too much. So, I've agreed to run the London office.'

'Really?'

'Yep. No more roaming Europe looking for adventure sports.'

'How will you like that?'

'I'm growing to the idea.' He smiled so tenderly that it was all I could do to not reach over and kiss him.

I took a large sip of wine instead.

'This means you'll be able to slip back into your old life too.'

My stomach clenched. He was referring to my nights out with the girls, the partying and all that. Did he think that was all I wanted forever? Did he think me so superficial? Obviously, he did.

'Oh, right. Yes, of course.' What could I say? No, you're wrong Liam, I don't want that life anymore. Would he believe me? Did I believe it myself?

Liam toyed with his wine glass. 'Shortly I'll be searching around for a place to live not far from London.'

I forced down a bite of chicken. 'There's plenty of places that are semi-rural and within good travelling time to London, though they'll be expensive.'

'I quite like the idea of staying in one place actually. With Gran becoming ill and Dad retiring, it's kind of a catalyst.'

'Like a sign that you should change your life, too, and settle down a bit?' Snap. I've been getting the same signs, mate!

'I've been travelling for ten years now, and I've loved it, but I can't do it forever. I don't want to do it forever, and dad deserves a rest.'

'Do you think you can though, seriously? I mean, it'll be hard to stay in one place after all those years of travelling the world.'

'No. I think I'll be all right. I wouldn't mind a place that is mine to call home.'

'And working in London? That's not easy.'

'Yes, I know, but it'll be only for the short term anyway.'

'Next you'll be thinking of marriage and kids.' I laughed nervously.

'Maybe I will. I've never ruled it out. I'd like to be a father.'

I nearly choked on a piece of tomato. The thought

of Liam being married and some woman having his kids made me want to retch the delicious food all over his lap.

I drained the rest of my wine.

Liam refilled my glass and added a little to his own. 'I have plans beyond the magazine. When Gary takes over in a few years I want to leave and focus on something else—something that has been on my mind for a long time now.'

'Oh? Can you share your plans?'

'It's nothing set in stone yet, but I'd like to build an adventure park.'

I stared at him. If he'd said he wanted to build a pyramid I couldn't have been more surprised. 'An adventure park?'

'Yes. Don't look so shocked.' He grinned. 'I've had my eye on a Grade listed house in Cornwall. It has eighty-seven acres.'

'You want to build another Alton Towers?'

'No, no. Nothing on that scale. Cornwall has ideal weather, so I was thinking along the lines of a water park, a playground and gardens. So, the adults can have a wander around the gardens while the kids played. What do you think?'

'I'm not sure.' If he'd mentioned plans to create a sky diving centre in Jamaica I'd have understood, or buy a yacht and sail around the world, I'd have thought that reasonable since it would be along the lines of what he's been doing for the last ten years. But an adventure park?

'You're the first I've told about it.'

I was the first? I stared at him in shock. He had confided in me before anyone else! I felt all giddy inside at the privilege. He must trust me enough to mention something as important as this. Then, I wasn't likely to go around telling everyone when I was no longer working for him, now was I? He hadn't taken a huge gamble after all. I pushed a slice of pepper around my plate. 'Don't we have enough theme parks in England, though? Will it be viable?'

'This won't be full of rides like the others. I don't want to go down that route. Let me show you, I have paperwork to back up my madness.' He chuckled and left the table.

But where did I fit in all this? Why did I feel like he was talking in riddles, hinting at things but not really saying anything I could grab hold of and build on?

Shit, what did it matter? I was leaving, wasn't I?

Returning a few minutes later, he placed a folder next to my plate. 'Have a look.'

Pushing my plate aside, I opened the folder. The first page was a real estate promotional flyer about a Grade listing manor house.'

Liam leaned closer, filling my nose with his cologne, and it took all my will power to concentrate on the contents of the folder. 'That's the house. I'll renovate it and live in one side of it. The other parts of the house I'll open to the public, along with intensive gardens. I want to put in a lake and fill it with fish so kids can learn how to fish and all that sort of thing. Everything, the activities and attractions, will have a water theme.'

I flipped over to the next page and studied a diagram of the acreage and drawings of attractions. 'This is a huge project.'

'I know.' Liam speared a slice of cucumber and popped it into his mouth.

'Have you done a financial report? I mean, will it be worth the money invested?'

'Yes, I have. I think it will be viable and hopefully profitable within five years. Summer in Cornwall can be as hot as the Mediterranean. Climate change is making England hotter each year. If I can build a water park, gardens, and so forth. I think, no, I know I can grab a share of the tourist industry.'

'I see.' I flipped over more pages.

'Remember, this isn't going to be a huge scale operation like some of the leading theme parks. It's not going to cost families a fortune to visit. I aim to target those who have already come down south for a holiday and want a break from the beach. This will be a day-tripper's experience.' He sipped his wine, watching for my reaction. 'You don't think it's a promising idea?'

'I can't say, Liam.'

'Course you can. You're intelligent; you have opinions.'

Why was he getting so uptight? What did he expect from me?

He pushed his plate away. 'I don't want to be stuck in London forever, or I'll go mad. This will give me something to do and something to look forward to, until Gary takes over the office.'

'I suppose I'm just surprised, that's all. It's not every day someone you know says they are opening an adventure park. It's not as if you said I'm buying a new car.'

'This is extremely important to me. It's my future.'

At least *he* had one.

Liam relaxed back into his chair and sipped his wine. 'You think I'm a fool, don't you?'

'No. No, I don't.' I smiled. 'Everyone must have something in their life, some goal to reach for.'

'What's yours?'

'I've no idea.' I chuckled but felt stupid. It wasn't in the least bit funny.

'Can I show you the house tomorrow? I'd like your opinion.'

I glanced at the photo of his derelict manor house and panic gripped me. No. I didn't want to see where he was going to live, where he planned to raise a family.

My chest constricted.

I couldn't breathe.

How brilliant, he was the one with high blood pressure, but I was the one going to have a heart attack! And in front of Liam. Shoot me now.

Chapter Nineteen

I scrapped back my chair. I needed air. I need to get out of the house and away from him.

'Katie? What's the matter?' Liam stood and touched my arm.

'N-Nothing.' I edged away. Enough. I could stand no more. Now was the time to tell him. 'I can't do this.'

'Do what?' Liam scowled, and so he should, he had no idea what plagued me, silly man. He must think I'm not right in the head.

'I have to leave. I'm sorry.' I headed for the hallway. I'd get my stuff and go.

'Leave?' Liam followed me. 'Why? What's wrong?'

At the bottom of the stairs I turned, angry, upset and plain tired of it all. 'I can't work for you anymore.' There. I'd done it.

'But why?' His gorgeous eyes widened in puzzlement.

'Because I can't.' I went up two steps, but he grabbed my arm before I could go any further.

'Katie, for God's sake speak to me.'

'No, Liam, just let me go.' Tears filled my eyes. Shit, crying in front of him was not clever.

'You're not going anywhere until I know what's going on. I thought we were friends, that you liked working with me?'

'That's the problem.' My chin wobbled. I blinked hard to stop the flood.

'What do you mean?'

With a plop, I sat down hard on the third tread. I might as well be truthful. I was leaving anyway so what did it matter if he knew I was in love with him? I'd already made a fool of myself; I might as well complete the process.

Liam hunkered down in front of me, his gaze soft with concern. Oh God, he was so lovely. The lump in my throat grew bigger.

I gave in to temptation and gently cupped his cheek with my hand, savouring the feel of his skin against mine. 'I've developed feelings for you.' I smiled weakly; my heart shattered into a squillion pieces that no amount of glue would ever put right. 'Not very professional of me, is it?'

'That is why you're leaving?'

'Yup.' I took a deep, shuddering breath. 'That's it in a nutshell.'

'You can't go because of that.'

'Yes, I can. It's hell. You have no idea.'

He took my hand and kissed my palm. I lost all sense of reality.

'What if I said I had feelings for you too?'

I stared, gob-smacked. He couldn't. Surely, I was hearing only what I wanted to hear.

Liam stood, pulling me up with him. 'Lets' go and sit down so we can talk.'

208

We both turned as one when the front door opened, and Meghan entered the house. She stopped and stared at our joined hands.

Heat rose to my cheeks, but Liam only held my hand tighter and faced his mother. 'You're home early.'

'Yes. Gran was having a few tests done so there was no point me sitting in an empty room for hours. Is-is everything all right here?'

Liam nodded and glanced at me. 'It will be. We're off out. We have some things to discuss.' He gestured me to go upstairs. 'Grab something warm, Katie. We'll go for a drive.'

'Have you eaten?' Meghan's gaze swept between us, confusion in her eyes.

Liam let go of my hand and headed down the hall. 'Yes. But we haven't cleaned up. I'll do it when we get back.' He disappeared into the kitchen, likely to reclaim the folder of his future plans.

I turned and headed upstairs, wondering if this all was some kind of sick dream. Did he really say he had feelings for me? Could such a thing happen? I needed a stiff drink—several of them. Maybe tranquillisers too.

Numb, I collected a jacket and my bag and made it back to the front door without falling down the stairs. Liam shrugged on a lightweight wind jacket, smiling at me the whole time. I couldn't smile back. I couldn't do anything but stand there expressionless like a shop mannequin.

'Ready?' He asked, taking the keys from his pocket.

'What did your mum think?'

'I've no idea. It's none of her business yet.'

I allowed him to take my hand and lead me out of

209

the house. We remained silent as we walked to the car, climbed in and drove away.

After all the days of wondering and worrying, longing to speak freely, now I had the chance only my brain wouldn't work. Thoughts whirled through my mind, sweat broke out on my upper lip, and I was sure a migraine was building.

Why didn't he speak?

I replayed the scene at the bottom of the staircase. I analysed his voice tone, the message in his eyes. Could I hope, truly hope it was real? Had my luck changed?

I had no idea where we were when Liam parked beside some lane overlooking the sea. Rain splattered the windshield, cocooning us in the car. Tension thickly coated the space between us.

Liam unbuckled his seatbelt and turned to me. We were inches apart, and when he looked into my eyes, I saw the same questions in his expression that I had.

'Well...' He gave me a wry smile.

I returned his smile, not trusting myself to speak.

'This is a bit of a shock, isn't it?'

'Which bit?' I croaked.

'All of it.' His fingers drummed the steering wheel. 'I never expected this.'

'Nor me.'

'I'm not one of those bosses who tries it on with his staff. I'm not some pervert.'

'I know.' I frowned. Is that what he believes I think of him?

He shifted in his seat, staring out the obscured windscreen. 'I'm not taking this well, Katie. I didn't go looking for a relationship. I was too busy. Never expected it to happen…'

I could feel his anxiety. My poor darling man. My

heart, the soft pathetic organ that it was, broke again, this time for him. Meeting me must have had the same impact as a sledgehammer hitting his Gran's best china.

'What are your thoughts?' he whispered.

My thoughts. Heavens, even I didn't understand my thoughts. I looked down at my hands clasped in my lap. 'I thought you didn't feel the same as I did.'

'I tried not to.' He sighed and flicked on the wipers to clear the view a bit. 'The last thing I wanted was to appear one of those lust-filled employers who chased skirts all day. I'm not an affair type of man.'

Good to know.

The silence lengthened between us, and I knew I had to do some talking of my own. So far, I hadn't given him much. I quietly cleared my throat, took a deep breath and plunged in. 'Liam.'

'Yes?'

'I don't want you thinking that I do this all the time. Falling in love I mean. I don't. And never with my boss.'

'I'm pleased to hear it.'

'Did you think I did?' I gaped.

'Not really.'

'But you had suspicions?' My eyes widened. This wasn't good.

'No…'

'Be honest now.'

'Well, I know you're not some saintly virgin.'

'True, but I'm not a slut either.'

'Oh, I know that.' He studied the rain pelting the windscreen.

'But?'

He shrugged one shoulder, looking decidedly uncomfortable. 'You party hard by all accounts.'

211

'So? It doesn't mean I sleep around.' Sheesh! Where did he get off putting two and two together and coming up with fourteen billion?

'I didn't say you did.'

'I haven't slept with someone for over a year.'

'You don't have to tell me anything.'

'I want you to know.' I turned away. Marvellous. This wasn't going as I expected, which was us falling into each other's arms. Just once couldn't I have a Hollywood moment? Was it too much to frigging ask?

Liam reached over and grasped my hand. 'I'm sorry. I'm a dickhead. I think I'm just jealous. I hate the thought of anyone being able to touch you.'

My throat thickened with emotion. I simply nodded in agreement. My thoughts were a mess. Was it possible for someone to simply love me as I was?

'Katie?'

I moved slightly, just enough to show him my face, though I kept my lashes lowered to hide my teary eyes.

He tilted my chin up. 'Look at me.'

Summoning the last reserves of my courage, I looked at him. Ever so slowly his head lowered, and his lips met mine gently, almost reverently. My whole body sighed at the touch.

'Darling Katie.' He rubbed his nose against mine, his lips whispering over my mouth. 'You have no idea what you've done.'

'Done?' I frowned. 'You can stop talking now. I much prefer your kisses.'

'You've turned my very ordered life upside down.' He softly nibbled my bottom lip.

'And that's bad?' I sighed, aching for more of his touch.

He chuckled. 'I'm sure I'll get used to it.'

I pulled back slightly, wanting to see his eyes. 'This isn't something light and-and trivial. Meeting you has changed my life. Changed *me*.'

'Good. I'm glad, because it's done the same to me. I tried to pretend it wasn't happening, that I wasn't attracted to you, but nothing worked.'

'You never responded to any of my signals.'

'I was your boss. I didn't want you to think of me as some creep who wanted a quick fumble in the car or something.'

'And now?'

'And now I still want more than a quick fumble.' He winked, his hands encircling my waist.

'I'm being serious.'

'So am I.'

'Liam!' I needed him to be serious. 'This was important. I want a relationship that will last. I am tired of games, of meaningless involvement.'

He let me go and threaded his fingers through mine suddenly solemn once more. 'If I told you that I've fallen in love with you, would you believe me?'

My heart somersaulted like a Russian gymnast. Did he actually say he LOVED me? Instead of dying with happiness, I strove for calm, just in case I hadn't heard properly. 'If you spoke the truth, then I would believe anything you said. Why wouldn't I?'

'Because it's only been weeks since we met.'

'Where does it say that you have to know each other for years before you can love someone?'

'People expect—'

'Stuff people. I love you. I knew that by the end of the first week. Yes, it was lust at first, but then as we spent more time together, and learnt more about each other, I knew I was falling in love with you. And I

213

was as miserable as sin about it.'

He lifted one hand to gently run his fingertip across my lips. 'Miserable? I know all about that too. I could barely sleep knowing you were across the hall from me.'

'You never let me believe or hope that we could be more than just working partners.'

'I'm sorry. I was your boss. I couldn't. It seemed wrong, as though I was taking advantage.' He took my hand and held it.

'Did you read the signals I was giving out? Like on top of the mountain and in the sea yesterday?'

'Yes, of course I did. I'd have to have been blind not to. But as I've said, I didn't want to cross the employer line. I had to pretend I didn't see anything.'

'But you knew my feelings?'

'I guessed you were attracted to me.'

'And how did that make you feel?'

He grinned cheekily. 'Pretty amazing, actually.'

'Not trapped?'

'No, never that. I wanted to be intelligent and clever and witty and cool. For you.' He shrugged. 'I suppose that's a male thing, is it, that I wanted your interest?'

I couldn't help but to smile. 'Yes, very cave man. And it worked. I wanted you right from the start.' I gazed down at our joined hands, liking the comfort from such a simple gesture. 'Why did you hang up on me when I was out the other night? Did you think I'd forgotten you?'

'I was thinking that, yes, and a lot of other things. Such as you were back to your old ways and I meant nothing to you, nor did your job.' He flexed his neck, as if this heart to heart talking was uncomfortable for him. 'To be honest I was hurt that you were having a good time without me, and I was insanely jealous.'

'Thank you for your honesty. Would you believe that I was miserable the whole time I was out?' I shook my head at the strangeness of it all. 'Joanna persuaded me to go as she was sick of seeing me moping around the house waiting for you to call. I was missing you dreadfully.'

'And I you, sweetheart. I have never missed anyone in my life before, not like that. I didn't like feeling so…'

'Vulnerable?'

'Yes. Since meeting you I've felt a lot of things. Usually I'm in control of myself, but with you… Well, I've lost my mind.'

'And heart?'

'Definitely my heart,' he whispered.

I leaned forward and kissed him softly, savouring the freedom to do so. We kissed deeply, properly for the first time, and I wanted to cry at the beauty of it.

I was *finally* kissing Liam-the-gorgeous-Kennedy, and it was bloody magnificent!

Gradually, lovingly we parted, but kept touching each other as if making sure it was real. I knew I would never grow tired of being near this man. For the rest of my life I wanted the liberty to caress him, to be the one he turned to for comfort and love. I could feel my heart mending piece by piece. 'I can't believe you feel the same as me.'

'Come here.' He clicked back his seat, making more room away from the steering wheel and then carefully dragged me over onto his lap.

Cuddling up to him, feeling his powerful arms around me was breath taking. If this was heaven on earth, then I was going to sell tickets. Everyone should be able to feel this wonderful.

Liam cupped my face and we stared into each other's eyes. He smelt amazing; the soft spicy cologne he wore filled my nose until I was high on it.

I arched into him, and his hands captured my waist and slid up my back, pulling me even closer until my breasts were squashed flat to his chest.

As his mouth sought mine again, I reached up and wrapped my arms around his neck, keeping him close, but wanting him even closer. His tongue stroked mine, exploring my mouth and one of his hands slipped down to my bum, where he gripped and pressed me in against him. I was on fire from the inside out. A burning coil of desire flared within the pit of my stomach, consuming me. As close as we were it wasn't enough, I wanted more—I wanted everything of him.

A smile escaped me as I felt his erection. I had no doubt now that he was attracted to me just as much as I was to him. I pulled up his shirt and ran my hand over his flat stomach and up his chest, lightly brushing his nipples and then I ventured lower to the waistband on his jeans. I popped the stud and lowered the zipper slowly.

'Katie…' He took my face between his hands and kissed me thoroughly, deeply as if he couldn't get enough of me. He kissed my neck, his hands running over my shoulders and then down to pull up my shirt. I arched into him as his hands found my breasts, caressing me. We kissed, our breath hot and heavy. The desire was clear in his eyes, etching his face and I smiled inwardly, revelling in the joy of this moment.

Liam Kennedy wanted to have sex with me, and I wasn't even perfect.

What's more, he had said the L.O.V.E. word.

Thank God.

Chapter Twenty

We came up for air a long time later. Although we didn't go all the way, we went pretty far and nearly needed a compass to get back. The car's windows were fogged up, and laughing, I put my hand up against it in 'Titanic's Rose style'. Though I wouldn't have swapped Liam for Leo if you'd paid me big money.

My insides were as warm and gooey as a melted toffee dessert.

I, yes *me, moi, Katie Olivia Edwards*, had just been making out with one ridiculously hot man. I couldn't stop gazing at him, adoring him.

'I haven't made out in a car since I was about twenty.' Liam grinned, adjusting his clothes and flexing his back. 'I'd forgotten how uncomfortable it is.'

'When was your last girlfriend?' This would be interesting. I was such a nosy cow.

He gave me a quizzical look. 'Why bring that up now?'

'I'm interested. I want to know everything about

you, the good, bad and indifferent.' I gave him a saucy wink. 'Tell me your secrets, Mr Kennedy.'

Liam shook his head and laughed. 'You are funny. I love your humour.'

'I hope it's not all you love about me.'

'No, not all,' he murmured and kissed me tenderly.

'So? Last girlfriend?' I wasn't going to let him wriggle off this particular hook.

'Um…Well, it was about two years ago. I was seeing someone for about two months, but she was a medical student and I was travelling, we never saw each other.'

'And before that?'

'Before Jen, I went out with Caroline for eight months, but I think she was a little crazy. She was always angry or upset about something and would never tell me what it was. She had issues.' He looked bemused and then shrugged. 'Before those two I had a dry patch of a few years, then a couple of one-night stands and—'

'What about a deep love?'

He thought for a moment. 'I can't honestly say I've had a real love. I've always been too busy, too focused on other things. The ones I've been out with were more for the physical side. Does that make me a bad person? I never really wanted a relationship that might hinder my career. I guess that's why I picked girls who were not easy, exactly, but they didn't want anything more either.'

'Okey-dokey.' I held my hand up to stop him. 'That'll do just lovely, thank you. I don't need to hear anymore.' And I didn't. I was secretly thrilled he had no one who's been the love of his life. I wanted that job.

He took my hand and played with my fingers.

'And your previous boyfriends?'

'Not worth the words really. And definitely not as many as you may think I've had.'

'Shall we drop the subject?'

'Definitely.' I scrambled back to my own seat with a laugh. 'What's the date?'

'Um August…fifth?'

'Right, for as long as we are together, we are going to go parking on this date every year.'

Wickedness flared in his eyes. 'Is that a promise?'

'Absolutely.'

'Even when we're old and grey and using Zimmer frames?'

'Even then.' I gazed at him. He wanted us to grow old together. Now that was commitment right there on a platter. 'I hope we live so long you'll forget our children's birthdays.'

'But I'll always remember this date.' He said, his tone serious, his eyes loving.

I nodded, too emotional to speak.

Liam kissed me. 'I love you.'

'And I love you, very much.'

'I think we're going to be good together, Katie. I can feel it.'

I preened like a peacock. 'No, not just plain good. Lord, no. We're going to be so blissfully happy people will be sick with jealousy just by looking at us. Hallmark will want us to write their cards for them. Therapists will use our love as a guide to others.'

'You are crazy.' He slid his seat into place and gave me a stunning smile. 'That was the first thing that attracted you to me, your ability to make me laugh.'

'Champion. It had to be the clown factor. It

couldn't be I was dazzling you with my beauty and startling wit.'

'Um, well, of course I was astounded by those too.'

'Liar!' I playfully punched his arm as he started the car.

'It's true.' He paused to gaze at me. 'You are beautiful and clever.'

I sighed happily, whether it was fact or fiction didn't matter. I know he meant it, and that was enough for me.

'I would like to meet your family.' Liam said, reversing the car. It was getting late and nearly dark.

'Okay. They aren't too scary. Well, my sister can be, but she's a lovable freak.'

'Would you like to meet Gran tomorrow?'

'Yes, thank you, I would. I've been wanting to.'

'I didn't want to ask before in case you thought it unprofessional.' He wiped a hand over his face. 'You've no idea how unprofessional my thoughts have been regarding you.'

'They couldn't have been worse than mine. I don't know how I survived Cumbria.'

'Ah, Cumbria.' He gave me a saucy look. 'You were amazing in Cumbria. Every test I threw at you, you grabbed it with both hands and wrung the life from it.'

'Test?'

'Yes.' He took his eyes off the road for a second to give me a clear look, all joking gone. 'Over dinner that first night and breakfast the next morning you came across as though this job was a little beneath you.'

'I never thought that!' I was amazed by his words, and that he thought such a thing.

'It's the impression I got. So, I thought I'd throw you in at the deep end and see if you would sink or swim. I didn't want to work with someone who didn't give a crap about the job. No matter what Karen said, I'd rather be on my own than lugging a dead weight.'

'I see.' How strange he thought that. I obviously didn't hide my feelings at all well. 'You were right. In a way, I didn't really care about the job. You see I had just left a horrid pervert boss. I wanted to take a holiday, recharge my batteries and then look for a different kind of job, one which I might find more interesting than what I'd been doing. I didn't want to be a personal assistant again. Too many bad memories. The last thing I expected was to land straight into another P.A. position.'

'Why did you take it then?'

I stared out at the passing dark countryside. 'I took it because of the money, I suppose, and security. My friend Joanna, always the sensible one, convinced me it would be a good thing to do. The travel bit excited me too.' Lord, I did sound shallow.

'Well, I'm glad you arrived in Cumbria. That decision you made changed my life.'

'And mine.'

He held my hand and steered with his other. 'No regrets?'

'How could I possibly have regrets? I have you.'

We were silent for a while and then Liam glanced at me before staring back at the road. 'After we visit Gran tomorrow, we could drive to North Cornwall and I'll show you the house and lands for the adventure park.'

'When do you think you'll put in an offer?'

'After you've seen it.'

I stared at him. Wow. 'Why does that make a

difference if I've seen it or not?'

'Well, I might be rushing it a bit, but I'd like to think one day you might want to be living there with me.'

Gobsmacked. There was no other word for how I felt.

I reached over and kissed his cheek. I loved this man so much it was a physical pain. 'Thank you.'

'For what?'

'For not being scared to think of commitment.'

He pulled the car over onto the side of the road and looked at me. 'Commitment doesn't scare me. When I said I loved you I meant it. To me, love means sharing your life with that person. What is there to be scared of?'

'Plenty apparently. Ask any fella in the street.'

He frowned. 'I'm not just anyone, Katie. I want us to be together as a couple.'

'I do too.'

'When Karen rang me today and said you were leaving, I thought I'd stop breathing. It was one of the worst feelings I'd ever had. I turned the car around and drove straight back, wondering how on earth I could convince you to stay.'

'I didn't know Karen had rung you.' Maybe she wasn't such a sergeant-major after all?

'She knew I didn't want to lose you as a P.A. I'd told her and dad how happy I was with you. Only they didn't know it went deeper than just employer and employee. Even I didn't want to believe it at first.'

Sighing, I caressed his hand. 'I wanted to leave because I've been so upset. Sick at heart really, thinking I'd never have your love, that I was destined to be some loveless loser all my life. I had decided to go home because it hurt too much spending time with you and not being able to *be* with you, if you know what I mean.'

'Of course, I know. I've been having the same fight inside myself.'

'To be honest, from the first moment I met you I didn't want to be your personal assistant. I just wanted to be your lover, your friend…'

'The first moment *I* met *you* I couldn't believe my luck. A gorgeous personal assistant. I hoped you had brains to go with your sexy smile.'

'My smile is sexy?' No one had ever said that to me before.

'Well, not at first, as you looked petrified. Did you think I was some hard-faced bastard?'

I laughed. 'No, not at all. The opposite. You hit me for six. So striking and so male. I wanted to fall into your arms. I nearly died when I realised you'd be my boss. Don't you know it is just *sad* to fancy your boss?'

'Really? I think that goes the same for the other way around too.' He laughed.

'But, beyond all the lust and everything, you helped me to see my life in a clearer way. I didn't realize how mundane my life had become. Oh, I suppose I might have changed eventually, but it might have taken years.'

'I didn't do anything, Katie. You became aware of what you wanted all by yourself. I just happened to be there.'

'Without you I would never have gone hiking, horse riding, fishing. There's an entire world out there and I didn't see it. Yes, I was restless, bored, needing a change and you gave me the opportunity to step outside my comfort zone.'

'I have a feeling you would have found your feet eventually. Maybe you needed to find someone who would love you no matter what and reassert your confidence.' Liam kissed my palm. 'I'm not a hero in shining armour.'

'I know. I don't want you to be. I simply wanted to thank you for opening my eyes.'

'Well, you've done the same for me too, you know.' He kissed me for several delicious minutes and then raised his head to smile at me. 'You don't want to work for me anymore?'

'I'm not sure. Actually…no, I don't think I do, at least not as a personal assistant.'

'Okay…'

'I want to study photography properly.'

'Photography.' He smiled. 'That sounds rather good.'

My heart swelled so much I thought it'd pop like a balloon inside my chest. 'Perhaps I can do that while you run the magazine from the London office, as you'll have Karen to help you. I won't be needed there.'

'Are you sure?'

'Positive. If it suited you, perhaps you could move into my flat…' I held my breath waiting for his answer. 'Just a suggestion of course.' I quickly added.

'Seems great idea to me. I'll need a London base and I want to be with you. It's a perfect solution.'

'Honestly?' Was Liam really going to move in with me? If I woke up in the morning and all this was a slap-in-your-face dream I would kill myself.

'Honestly.'

'And then, later I could help you set up your adventure park.'

Warmth filled his eyes and he reached over again

to kiss me lovingly. 'Thank you.'

'For what?'

'For believing my scheme isn't stupid.'

'Nothing you'd ever do would be stupid.'

Liam cupped my cheek, and his thumb rubbed my bottom lip. 'Katie, I haven't got a crystal ball. I don't know what the future will bring, but I'm hoping this is the real thing between us.'

'Me too. It's all I want. *You* are all I want.'

We kissed for what seemed like forever until we both started to get cramps in our backs and necks from the uncomfortable position of leaning between the seats. For a while we sat quietly together, sometimes talking, sometimes enjoying the silence. Although the passion and desire throbbed between us, waiting to be explored, I also loved simply sitting with him. We would never get this time back again, this first innocent building frame where we learned more about each other without life's problems interrupting. I wanted to absorb this magical time of us being a new couple, of creating a foundation.

However, hours later as we travelled back to the house secure and confident in each other, I wondered what the night would bring. Sex? A gentle parting at the bedroom doors?

Bugger that.

I needed sex with Liam.

Chapter Twenty-One

At the house, we entered through the kitchen door and found Meghan placing some luggage next to the table.

She straightened and gave us a brief smile. 'Oh good, you're back. Fancy a cup of tea?'

'I'll put the kettle on.' Liam filled the kettle with water and flicked the switch.

I noticed the drying rack on the sink was stacked with our dinner plates and felt guilty for leaving a mess for Meghan. 'I'm sorry about dinner. You should have left that for me to wash up.'

Liam grabbed a tea towel and started drying plates. 'Yes, Mum, I told you to leave it.'

'Nonsense. I don't mind at all.' Meghan went into the hallway and brought through another large bag. 'Liam, I'm off in the morning. I'm going home to spend a few days with your dad. Gran's doctors say she won't be released to come home until the weekend. We'll come back on Saturday morning.'

He nodded. 'Right.'

'You'll see to her, won't you? Take in some nice

food and fruit for her. She won't eat much of the hospital stuff.'

'We'll visit her every day. I'll buy her some special treats.'

'She's not a dog, Liam.' Meghan snapped.

I stared from mother to son. Had we upset Meghan?

Liam thrust his hands into his jeans pockets. 'Gran will be fine, don't worry. I'll look after her.'

Meghan gave me a small, uncertain smile. I knew she was weighing up what had happened earlier between her son and me. The hand holding and the tears must have confused her, thrown her a bit. To her it would be all too soon, too abrupt and maybe even unethical? The whole employer and employee thing.

Liam took out clean cups. 'Katie and I will visit Gran in the morning.'

'Fine.' Meghan opened the door and then grabbed some of the luggage. 'I'm packing the car tonight as I want to leave by six in the morning.' She seemed a little on edge and couldn't really look us in the eyes.

I stared at Liam, trying to give him a message with my eyes and a slight twitch of my head. He had to talk to her and explain.

He nodded again in reply. 'I'll give you a hand, Mum.' He grabbed her bags and they left the house.

Taking a deep breath, I walked through to the lounge room and switched on the TV. The noise of some movie filled the silent room. Minutes ticked by. Nerves made me pace the floor. What if she didn't accept me? What if she talked Liam out of seeing me? My stomach churned. I closed the curtains in the front window, straightened some magazines on the coffee table, chewed the fingernail on my right pinkie, changed the channel on the TV and found a news bulletin, but for once the world news didn't interest me. The outside world didn't exist at that moment.

What was taking them so long?

If Meghan didn't approve of us, I didn't know what I'd do. Beg? Plead with her to change her mind? Liam was so close to his mother; would he listen to her over me? Oh God. Nausea rose, draining my happiness.

Finally, after another ten minutes of waiting I heard the kitchen door open and voices. I quickly sat on the sofa and pretended to be calm and interested in the news, which my blurred mind couldn't compute well and all I could understand was that some B-grade celebrity in America had been caught up a minor traffic offence. Like really, did anyone care about stuff like that? Was it worth being telecast around the world as 'important' news?

'Katie?'

I swung around to see Liam standing in the doorway. He smiled so lovingly my heart dipped in response. 'Is-is everything okay?'

'I think so.'

As he walked to the sofa I stood, searching his face for clues. 'Did you tell her?'

'Yes.' Liam encircled me in his arms, and I held him tight around the waist.

'And?' Lord, I felt like a teenager on my first sleep over at my boyfriend's house.

'She was shocked at first. It worried her we had only known each other for a brief time, but after talking it through with her, she understands how I feel.' He let me go and as one we sat on the sofa; fingers interlocked. 'I even told her about my plans for the adventure park.'

'What did she say?'

'Not a lot at first, it surprised her. She imagined I would run the magazine for years.' He shrugged. 'She's going to talk to Dad about it all.'

'Where is she now?'

'Having a cup of tea in the kitchen and I suppose thinking over everything I said.' Liam rubbed his thumb over my knuckles. 'She kind of knew I had been a little different lately.'

'Yes, she told me at breakfast.'

'Oh, you two had a little talk, did you?' He gave me a wry smile and I reached over and kissed him lightly on the lips.

'She told me about your blood pressure too.'

'It's under control now.'

'But you're working too hard still.'

'Because I need to earn as much money as I can for the park.'

'Your health is more important, Liam.'

'I know. Things will change now. I have you to keep me in line. Come here.' He pulled me onto his lap, and I snuggled in close, nuzzling his neck, breathing in his scent of soap and cologne. Raising my head, his lips found mine and we kissed long and slow, exploring and tasting, becoming familiar with each other.

Liam broke the kiss to nibble the soft skin under my jaw. 'You know,' he whispered, 'I can't make love to you tonight, not with Mum sleeping across the hall.'

Disappointment flooded me. I tilted my head back so he could have access to my neck while his hand cupped my breast, teasing my nipple. 'Yes, I understand.'

'But tomorrow…' Liam said on sigh as he slipped his hand under my shirt.

'Yes. God yes…' I grabbed his face between my hands and kissed him like someone demented. Fire raced along my veins. My body ached for him to fulfil me.

The sound of water running and then a door being locked broke us apart, albeit reluctantly. I scrambled off Liam's lap and straightened my shirt and hair just as Meghan stuck her head around the door.

'I'm off to bed now. I'll probably not see you in the morning as I want to get off early.'

'Okay, Mum.' Liam walked over and kissed her cheek. 'Drive carefully.'

'I will.' She smiled at me. 'Goodnight, Katie.'

'Goodnight, Meghan.'

'Will you still be here at the weekend? Clive would like to meet you, I'm sure.'

Liam came to me and took my hand, a clear show of support. 'Yes, she'll still be here. I'm not letting her out of my sight.'

'Lovely. Well, goodnight.' Meghan closed the door on her way out.

I slumped onto the sofa. Had I passed her test? Did she like the idea of us together? I was unsure. She hadn't given me too much to work with.' Are you sure she's okay about us? She didn't seem happy.'

'Mum likes you; she told me.'

'Maybe she liked me more as your P.A. and not as your girlfriend?'

'Honestly, don't worry. She'll come around once she's had time to see us together and how happy we are. I've hit her with a lot tonight. I think she's more upset about me leaving the magazine and opening the park, than you and me.'

'What will your dad say about all this? It'll be a huge shock for him too.'

'He won't say nothing much about us, so don't worry. By the time he arrives here at the weekend, Mum will have talked his ears off about us and he'll be sick to death of hearing about it.'

'How do you think he'll react about the park?'

'That I don't know.' He took a deep breath. 'He's always encouraged us to follow our own interests. I think he'll be anxious I'm doing the right thing. I suppose that's what fathers do. Regarding the magazine, well I don't know how he'll react. I will devote two years to it until Gary can take over, but that's all. I need to live my own dream.'

'Your father will understand that, I'm sure. I hope he likes me.'

'Who couldn't like you?'

'Well, my math teacher never did and neither did our neighbour's dog when I was little.'

Liam laughed and crushed me into him. 'You are adorable, Katie Edwards.'

Chapter Twenty-Two

I woke from a deep sleep to kisses being lightly rained over my face. Opening my eyes, I smiled at Liam. 'Morning.'

'Morning, beautiful.'

That he'd called me beautiful on seeing me the minute I woke up earned him enough brownie points to last a good year.

Liam rested his body down the length of the bed. He wore only navy silk boxers and seemed very awake. 'You look warm and toasty in there.'

'I am.' I squinted around the room, which was lit by sunshine. 'What time is it?'

'After seven. Mum left an hour ago.' He was propped up on his elbow, with his head to one side and his other hand cupping my cheek. 'Do you want some breakfast or a shower or…'

'Or you perhaps?' I grinned.

'Or me. Hmm…Yes I think I could accommodate you.'

'I'm sure you could, but first let me up so I can clean my teeth.'

He laughed and rolled onto his back as I climbed out of bed. 'Where's the spontaneity in that?'

'Spontaneity, my ass.' I laughed and padded across the hallway to the bathroom, glad that I wore my best PJs of pink satin.

'Are you always so coarse in the morning?' he called from the bed.

'That and more,' I answered back, feeling wonderfully alive.

It was funny how nervous excitement tingled in my stomach as I cleaned my teeth. In several seconds I'd done with my teeth, washed my face and was hurrying back to bed.

Liam was under the covers with his hands behind his head and a cheeky smile playing on his lips. He looked like he was doing a cover shoot for a bed company.

Suddenly shy, I held back a moment. He was so gorgeous and breath taking, like a dream, really. It was hard for me to think it was real.

'You okay?'

I nodded, all stupidly emotional. 'I never thought…'

'Come here, sweetheart.'

I kind of slid into the bed like a melted marshmallow and at once Liam pulled me into his arms and kissed away all doubts, not that many were building.

'I love you, Katie.' The earnest tone in his voice was mirrored in his eyes and at that point I knew this man meant everything to me. I kissed him tenderly, reverently, hoping to show him just how much I cared for him.

My body arched into his, moulding to his shape as though it was built for that purpose, and it was. Never had I felt so complete, so right as I did at this moment.

Our kisses grew deeper, more heated and urgent. I sucked in air, desperate for more of him, my hands sliding over his body. Liam tugged my top off and my breasts were free for him to torture with sensual sucking and licks. Against my thigh, his erection showed me exactly how aroused he was, and empowered by it, I slipped my fingers inside his boxers and slid them down.

'Katie…' Liam moaned into my mouth as we kissed again, our bodies desperate to be complete. 'Katie, I want to go slow, but I don't think I can.'

I smiled at him, loving him so much. 'We have the rest of our lives to go slow.' I took his bottom lip between my teeth and stroked his penis, loving the silky feel of it in my hands.

He groaned and quickly pulled off my PJ bottoms. 'Condom.' He reached for the bedside table, but I was closer and got it first.

I dangled it in front of him. 'Came prepared, did you? What if I had said no?'

'Would you have?' He ran the tip of his tongue between my cleavage and headed downwards, wiping the smile off my face as heat invaded every part of my body. We both knew I wouldn't have said no in a million years. I will want this man when I'm in a nursing homes for old aged pensioners.

Liam knelt between my legs, his fingers drawing tickling circles around my bellybutton. 'Want to say no, sweetheart?'

I laughed and sat up, wrapping my arms around him. 'I just might.' I fell backwards pulling him with me, but he rolled over onto his back and suddenly I was on top of him. Moving down the bed, I left a trail of kisses down his flat stomach then I ripped open the condom and gently rolled it on.

Before Liam had a chance to move, I straddled him, taking him deep within me. Pleasure washed over me as I saw the same response in his expression.

I rolled my hips softly, and Liam matched the movement only for a few moments before he flipped me onto my back and cuddled me in his arms. Opening my legs wider, I arched my hips up to meet his thrusts. The tantalising pressure built and this time it seemed more intense than any other time for me. Obviously being truly in love with someone made the experience so much greater and personal. I now knew the difference between sex for the body and sex for the mind. There was no holding back for me. I wanted to give everything I had to Liam.

I brought his head down to kiss him. 'I love you,' I whispered just as he gave a powerful thrust and I was sent over the edge into a white abyss. Liam tensed and then shuddered. I wrapped my legs around him tighter, hoping that the experience for him was as wonderful as it was for me.

Liam gazed down at me and smiled, and I sighed in relief. He kissed me tenderly and then rolled onto his side, hugging me to him. 'Okay?'

'Perfect.' I lay my head on his shoulder, astounded by the enormity of the happiness that flowed through me.

'Do you know we can do this for the rest of our lives?' he joked, running his fingers up and down my spine.

'Sounds like heaven, doesn't it?'

He kissed my nose and slid out of bed. 'Back in a second.'

I sat up and stretched. Satisfaction seeped out of

every pore. The grin wouldn't leave my face. Every woman should start their day by making love with a man who could win the Sexiest Man Alive award. Closing my eyes, I replayed our lovemaking in my mind. It had been natural and right, perfect in every way. Energy cursed through me. My body hummed, was keyed up, excitable.

I heard the toilet flush and then the shower run. Smiling, I tip-toed across to the bathroom and found the door unlocked. As quiet as a proverbial mouse I entered the bathroom and opened the shower cubicle. 'Fancy sharing some of that water?'

Liam turned and grinned. 'Want to wash my back?'

'Certainly.' I stepped into the flow of water and took the soap from him. I proceeded to torment his body in slow, sensuous movements, making sure I didn't miss one inch of him. And there was one area that needed exceptional attention. Before long, he'd lifted me up to wrap my legs around his waist and we were at it like rabbits again!

'Condom, Liam!' I breathed, gripping his wet shoulders.

'Bugger it.' He licked the water off the tip of my nose.

'What?'

'We both want kids.'

I leaned back, blinking water out of my eyes. He was a fast mover. 'Yes, but not now.'

'No?'

'No. I want time for just you and me first and probably a wedding somewhere in there too.'

'Rightio then.' In a few deft movements he turned off the shower, threw some thick towels onto the floor and laid me down on them. 'Stay.' He dashed out again and returned seconds later with a condom. 'Why aren't you on the pill?'

'Because I refuse to pop chemicals every day for years.'

'Fair enough.'

I looked up at him from my position of lying on towels on the bathroom floor. I had never done it on the bathroom floor before. How decidedly wicked! 'Are you going to stand there all day, sir?'

'By the end of today, my love, *you'll* be the one lucky enough to stand!'

I squealed with laughter as he pretended to ravish me. He thrust inside me as I went to speak again, cutting off my words about beds being soft…

Chapter Twenty-Three

I was singing to a Cold Play song when Liam pulled off the road and into a rutted driveway that cut between open fields. We were along the north coast of Cornwall somewhere. I should have paid more attention to the signs but couldn't be bothered. I'd have plenty of time later to know the route to the house, but right now I just wanted to wallow in the pleasure of being with this man who loved me.

After making love in the bath and then again eating breakfast, which in the end didn't get eaten, we finally made it to the hospital. We spent a lovely morning with Liam's Gran. Jane Kennedy delighted me. She still owned a faded beauty, which reminded people that not so long ago she'd been a stunner. I took to her the moment we met, and I think the feeling was mutual. For two hours we sat and drank tea, eating the apple pie Liam bought for her. Everything was discussed, childhood through to the present. Jane knew how to hold a conversation and keep her guests entertained, but she also knew how to listen, too, and she had listened to Liam talk of his plans for the adventure park with impressive pride.

As we left her to have a nap, Jane took my hand and welcomed me into the family. That touching moment brought tears to my eyes and I had kissed her papery cheek in gratitude and affection. No matter what the future held for Liam and me, I would always be grateful for that kind welcome from Jane.

'This drive leads up to the main house,' Liam said as we bumped and careened over potholes deep enough to swallow mountain dogs whole. 'I want you to see the house first.'

'If you are successful in your bid to buy the house, this driveway has to be the first priority,' I murmured as I was thrown towards Liam for a second time. 'Otherwise, we'll need a back brace just to leave the house.'

'Yes, it's shit, I know.'

I stared at him. It was the first time I'd heard him swear.

He frowned. 'What?'

'I've never heard you swear before.' I laughed.

'Well, I've always been your boss, it didn't seem appropriate, but now I'm your boyfriend I can relax a bit.' He grinned. 'I don't swear much.'

I gave him a superior look. I'd believe that when I see it.

Finally, we rounded a bend and a group of trees and there before us rose the house like some medieval manor, which it easily could have been to the uneducated. However, Liam had read to me the details of the house as we ate breakfast. The house was in fact early Victorian. The front façade looked regal, yet with an old-world charm. Dormer windows pierced the roof and large windows evenly occupied the first floor and on either side of the double door on the ground level. Former gardens were now neglected, but the form of them remained, and, with a bit of elbow grease and new plants, they would soon be returned to their former glory.

Liam cut the engine, staring at the house. 'The place is empty. So, we can have a look around if you want?'

'Sure.' I climbed out and gazed around. Brilliant sunshine warmed me and brightened the abandoned house, making it seem less of a derelict property and more of a sad home in need of a family.

God, hark at me for getting all fanciful.

I followed Liam to the first large window, and we peeked in. It appeared to be a formal front room.

'There are two wings, one on either side of the main rooms.' Liam stepped over weeds to the front door, which he rattled. 'Damn I wish I had a key.'

'Ring the real estate agent and see if they can come out.'

'They never turn up without three days' notice in advance,' he grumbled, going on to the next window.

'Ring them and try. It won't hurt.'

He brought his phone out and made the call while I peeked in more windows around the side. I liked the appearance of the rooms, although neglected they held a fragile beauty and begged to renovated. I wanted to be the one to do it. Suddenly, I wanted this house badly. It spoke to my heart. This was our house. Mine and Liam's. I stroked the stonework, and I don't know if it was because my senses were in overdrive or not, but I felt a connection.

A few minutes later, Liam joined me all smiles.

I hugged him. 'Well?'

'He just had an appointment cancellation, so he'll be here in an hour.'

'Told you.'

'Shut up.' Liam grinned and took my hand. We strolled around to the back of the house and explored the separate garage and outbuildings. We stood at the fence of the first field behind the buildings and stared off into the distance.

'Imagine that full of gardens and water rides, the laughter of happy kids…'

'I see horses for us to ride too.' I gave him a nudge in the ribs.

'Okay, and horses too. Ponies for children.'

I glanced up at him and slipped my hand through his arm. 'You really want this, don't you?'

'Apart from you, more than anything else in the world.'

His words filled my heart. What a perfect thing to say. 'It's a huge undertaking, Liam.'

'I know. It scares me a little, which I suppose is healthy.'

'Yes, it can never be taken for granted. You'll have to do thorough checks with the house, for damp and stuff.'

'Yes, of course.'

'We'll need a financial advisor, maybe even investors.'

'Yes. I've listed it all down in my planner. When we get home this afternoon, we can go through it all together.' He hesitated; his expression anxious. 'Honestly, what do you think of the place so far?'

I studied the property some more, really looked at each feature with an open mind. Could I live and work with Liam in Cornwall? Could I be happy this far away from my family? A warm funny feeling encircled my chest. Yes, I could see myself living there, making a home in that house with Liam and a few babies and a couple of dogs. I wanted to help him achieve his dream and be a part of it all. I wanted to not only share his life but yearn for the same things he did. I could rise to this challenge. Not only that, I could and would excel in finding my own dreams here. With Liam.

'Well?' Liam turned to me as we walked around the outbuildings once again, his eyes full of worry. 'I know there is a lot of work to be done. It'll likely take a year or so just for the plans to be approved in council and all that nonsense.'

I peered inside an old stable. Woodpigeons were nesting in the rafters. 'And there is the possibility of them saying no. Have you thought of that?'

'I have.' He sighed and some of the excitement left his face. 'I'll fight it if they do. I know this venture can be successful. I'll be environmentally friendly. I'll make sure the park benefits the community, not detracts from it.'

'Is there a community here? We seem so far from anyone else.'

'The local village to the east is five miles away, the rest are mainly small farms and Padstow isn't too far away. I know this can be a flourishing tourist park, which will bring money into this area.'

I remained silent, adoring the passion in his face. He wanted this so badly, and I was worried what would happen if it didn't work.

He kicked at a stone with the toe of his shoe. 'You don't like it, do you?'

I reached over and cupped his cheek. 'I adore it actually.'

'Really?' Hope flared in his eyes.

'Have you thought about acquiring a partner?'

'No. Not yet.'

'Well, I've been thinking.'

'You have?'

'I want to try new things, take opportunities.'

'What are you saying?'

'I know it's early stages for us, but I believe we will go the distance.'

He stared intently at me. 'Katie, what are you trying to say?'

I glanced around at the buildings, the open fields. My decision was made. 'I like it here, Liam. So much so that I'll sell my flat and use the money to invest in the park.'

'Katie, that's a huge undertaking. Your flat is your only asset.'

'I'll be investing in this glorious place and in you. How can that be wrong?'

'Are you sure?'

I smiled. 'I am completely sure.' I took a deep breath. 'I want you and this house, the park. I am selfish enough to want it all and I'll work hard to make it happen. I want us to have a future, Liam. And a future here seems a good start.'

'We'll be partners in every way. I promise. '

'Absolutely.'

He grabbed me into a bear hug that threatened to starve me of oxygen. 'You're wonderful. Thank you!' He kissed me repeatedly. 'You won't regret it. I'll make certain you won't have a minute's regret.'

'I know.' I pulled away and scowled into the distance.

'What's the matter?'

'I'm making sure there's no bloody mountains to climb.'

Liam laughed and swung me around. 'If, no, *when* we're successful I promise to buy you a house in the

Lake District and you can hike all the flat places you want.'

I playfully slapped his shoulder. 'You can hike. I'll take photos.'

'Hello there!' We looked around to find the property agent walking towards us.

I gave Liam a kiss. 'Come on then, let us view our future home.'

Epilogue

Four Years later

The noise of the crowd gradually grew silent as the sun sank below the horizon. I watched the last of the tourist busses depart and the odd family car until all had gone. Stillness enveloped the land. Summer was over.

I locked and left entrance gate and turned to wander through the gardens. I smiled at a couple of the employees, two young women, who were closing the kiosk. A young man, another employee, was busy collecting garbage and tidying the picnic area of litter.

Following the gravel path, I strolled past the aviaries of exotic birds and then past the reptile cabin, from inside I heard the keeper whistling. Beyond the extensive gardens, complete with several large fountains and small wading pools, I headed towards the farm animal enclosure. The cries of baby animals were heard long before I reached the farmyard area. I knew the person I sought would be here. It was his favourite place in all the world.

I was right. There inside the low fence, sitting amongst rabbits, chickens, piglets, lambs and ducks was Connor, my two-year-old son. I leaned against the fence as much as my pregnant stomach would allow. 'Hello, darling. Had fun?'

Connor, the image of his father, gave me a toothy smile. 'Look!' He held up a poor suffering piglet. 'Pig!'

'Yes, darling. Put him down now. He's tired. He's been playing with children all day.' I looked at Dave, one of the animal handlers as he entered the enclosure with a bucket of feed. 'Have you been stuck with Connor, have you?'

'Oh, he's no trouble, Katie. Liam was busy and didn't need this little fellow under his feet.' Dave ruffled Connor's hair. 'He helps me, don't you little guy?'

Connor scrambled to his feet and shepherded the animals. 'I help.'

'Do you want me to take him, Dave?' I asked.

'No, I'll bring him up to the house when I'm done.'

'Okay. I'll go and find Liam then.'

'He'll be down at the Water Jet. I think they're having trouble with one of the pumps.'

'Right, thanks.' I blew a kiss to Connor, who wasn't the least interested in his boring mum whenever there were baby animals to pat and kept walking.

Stifling a yawn, I flexed my shoulders. The tourist season had ended, and I was glad. We'd had a busy first season, and I hadn't been prepared for the amount of challenging work it would need to run a successful tourist park. That said, I did enjoy it. Seeing the relief on Liam's face as people flocked here and been worth every nervous moment. As a couple his worries and concerns had become mine, and visa-versa. We had developed a strong bond through love and friendship. Together we weathered the storms as well as rode the highs.

After eighteen months of dealing with the council, the park was approved. It took another year to build the site to the exacting standards Liam wanted. During that time, Liam stayed with the magazine until Gary came and took it off our hands. I completed a photography course and soon after we married in a small, but beautiful ceremony in London with all our family and friends present.

Our honeymoon was a few days in the south of France, and I fell pregnant almost immediately. My flat was sold, and we moved full time to Cornwall. Connor was born here amidst the house renovations and contractors. Despite the worry of getting the park up and running, I had never been happier. I knew Liam felt the same. Connor was a magical addition to our love. A precious gift, which strengthened our union.

'Hello, you.'

I turned around, surprised to see Liam stepping out from behind a curve in the path. 'I was on my way to see you.'

He kissed me and as always ran his hand over my bump. 'It looked like you were daydreaming to me.' He grinned. 'Where's our little man?'

'With Dave.'

'I should have known.' Liam wrapped his arm around my waist as we walked along. 'You look tired.'

'I am a bit. Is everything all right?'

'Yes, the pump on the water jet was playing up a

bit, but Harry and I sorted it out. I'll get a new pump for next season though.'

We paused by the entrance into the water slides and pools. Over three acres had been given to water rides and activities. Next to that was area for the horse and pony rides and then next to that, the jumping castles, which were in the process of being deflated. The sight saddened me.

I glanced at Liam, who watched the procedure with interest. 'It doesn't seem right, does it?'

'What, my love?'

'That everything is closing down. We've had six busy months and soon it'll be all quiet and peaceful.'

'The animals will still be here. They are never quiet.' He leaned his back against the gate and surveyed the parkland and gardens. 'I can't believe we did it, Katie.'

I nestled in close to him and looked back at the house, our home. 'But we did do it. And we did it well.'

His chest swelled. 'This has been the best summer of my life. I have you and Conner and a new baby on the way, and I saw our business succeed. Sometimes I think I have too much and something will happen to ruin it.'

I kissed his cheek. 'Nothing will ruin it, my love. I won't let it. We've worked hard for what we have. None of it came easy. Remember our first winter here? We had frozen pipes, leaking roofs, terrible heating.' I smiled remembering the time when I thought none of this would ever be possible.

A light came into Liam's eyes. 'Remember when we had the machines in to dig the drains and it rained for three weeks straight and everything was such a mess with mud two foot deep.'

'God, yes. It was a nightmare.' I hugged his arm. 'But we got through it all.'

'I couldn't have done it without you.'

I gave him a devilish look. 'Well, of course you couldn't have. Don't you know you've married the best woman in England?'

He winked cheekily. 'Maybe the best in the world.'

I gave a superior sniff. 'I wouldn't go that far. After all, I am only human.'

Liam laughed and crushed me to him. 'I love you, Katie Kennedy.'

AnneMarie Brear

AnneMarie Brear was born to Yorkshire parents, but grew up in Australia. Her love of reading fiction started at an early age with Enid Blyton's novels, before moving on into more adult stories such as Catherine Cookson's novels as a teenager. Living in England, she discovered her love of history by visiting the many and varied places of historical interest.

The road to publication was long and winding with a few false starts, but she finally became published in 2006. Since that time, Annemarie's had twelve novels and several short stories published. Her contemporary romance, *Hooked on You,* was a 2011 finalist for the international EPIC award.

However, currently, AnneMarie is writing only historical novels, mainly set in Yorkshire in the eras covering from Victorian to WWII and 1920s. Her books are available in ebook and paperback from bookstores, especially online bookstores such as Amazon, and also in audio and large print.

Annemarie Brear has done it again. She quickly became one on my 'must read' list. –The Romance Studio

http://www.annemariebrear.com (join her newsletter)
https://www.facebook.com/annemariebrearauthor
https://twitter.com/annemariebrear

Thank you for reading my books, if you feel inclined to leave a review on the different review sites, I'd be most grateful.

AnneMarie Brear

AnneMarie Brear

Printed in Great Britain
by Amazon